WICKED WARDEN

VICIOUS VIPERS MC 1

LYNN BURKE

WICKED WARDEN

I spend a decade running from the demons of my past until they show up at the Vicious Vipers MC compound in need of my help.

I failed to watch over the one woman who meant everything to me, even if she wasn't mine. But, I will not fail in protecting her daughter, despite the crime lords gunning for her.

She's feisty and fierce, and off limits, but damn if my body and mind aren't on the same page.

She might not think she needs looking after, but I will fulfill my promise to her father to keep her safe —even if the cost is my life for hers.

DEDICATION

For Golden & Cecile

CONTENTS

SHAUN

I finally had my freedom—from Dad, from his goons, and the two babysitters he'd sent off to college with me. PITA one and PITA two followed me everywhere, never allowing me a chance to breathe, thus the pain in the ass nicknames. I also left my cell phone behind since I knew the damn thing had a tracker tucked inside, thanks to Dad's anxiety about keeping me safe.

Not that I'd hear my phone where we were headed anyway.

The cool fall air nipped at my nose, and stomach fluttering, I hurried down the sidewalk, arm in arm with my best friend Krystal. We'd been giggling like kids rather than juniors in college ever since losing the two PITAs a half hour earlier.

She'd recently turned twenty-one, and although I had a few months before joining the legal drinking crowd, I'd jumped aboard the chance to live it up at a dance club that had recently opened in Boston's downtown—a place owned by her oldest cousin who'd promised me entrance without an ID.

Score.

Rather than wait in the line of scantily clad girls hoping to get past the huge-ass bouncer checking names off a list by the front door, we skirted down the alleyway alongside the old brick building.

Her cousin stood outside the back door, a cigarette dangling from his lips, his shoulders hunched against the cold air. "Fucking cold as balls out here," he growled as we clattered toward him in our heels and short skirts. "Hurry the fuck up."

"Sorry, Buddy," Krystal said, breathless as me from laughing and trying not to trip in our Jimmy Choos.

He frowned while dropping his butt and steeping on it, but kissed her cheek. "Shaun," he said, dipping his head toward me, knowing better than to get in my personal space.

Laughing, I grabbed him and planted a smooch on his cheek, holding my breath against the stench of stale cigarettes. "I gave my babysitters the slip, so

PDA won't get your hand or dick lobbed off for touching me."

"Good for you. Enjoy it while you can, love." Buddy pecked me back with a big grin and turned toward the door.

I'd been to enough of their family gatherings that he knew my shadows followed *in* the shadows at all times. Unless I got lucky like I did that night.

The thump of bass and warm air blasted us when we entered the private area of Buddy's club, the heavy door shutting with a clank behind us as we scurried after him. Thick carpet hushed our footfalls, and we passed a few closed doors on our way before stopping at his office to drop off our coats and purses.

A shorter trek down another hall brought us to a metal, windowless door.

"After you, ladies," Buddy said, pulling it open and gesturing us into the lounge.

Strobe lights flashed in the dark area, lighting up a sea of writhing bodies. The music, something techno and loud as hell, thumped through my body, making my feet itch to move with the beat. I couldn't stop smiling as warmth radiated throughout my entire body.

This is what freedom feels like...

"Drinks first!" Buddy shouted over the music, and Krystal and I both nodded, scurrying after him as he headed toward the bar on our right.

People crushed three-deep, waving cash as though it would get the attention of one of the five bartenders scrambling to serve them all, but the crowd parted like the Red Sea for Buddy.

He pulled us forward and leaned in close. "Get whatever you want—on me—and when you're ready to head home, meet me in the office. I'll grab an Uber to get you back to your apartment safe and sound just like the PITAs would."

"Thanks!" we both shouted, grinning like a couple of idiots, Krystal's cheeks flushed from excitement.

Free booze. Dancing. Maybe finding someone to sneak into my apartment—bed—for the night... If I could stay off the PITAs radar.

Buddy waved down a bartender and pointed at the two of us.

The bartender nodded, smiling yet frazzled-looking from the patrons clamoring for alcohol. "What can I get you?" she hollered, leaning over the bar toward us, her huge tits nearly spilling out of her tight as fuck shirt.

"Something fruity!" Krystal hollered back, holding up two fingers.

Minutes later, both of us gripping red, frothy drinks, we made our way to the dance floor. The liquor burned as I gulped a big swig, but I reveled in the rush, the thrill of not having anyone watch my every move. We bumped and ground our way into the thick of the crowd, and I got so damn caught up in my elation, I didn't care more than one person grabbed a handful of my ass.

Krystal and I ended up back to back, a couple of hotties grinding on our fronts as we danced, our drinks held high in the air. Sweat soon beaded on my forehead and trickled between my cleavage and down my back, but the night had just begun.

An hour and two drinks later, we stood breathless at the crowd's edge, still shimmying away. My smile plastered to my face as the guy I'd been dancing with most of the night approached, two bottles of beer in hand.

His dark eyes drank me in with the type of lust I'd been hoping to find that night. Getting laid was a sure bet with the guy, whatever his name was, and about time, too. It had been months since I'd gotten any thanks to the damn PITAs lurking in the shadows every minute of the damn day.

The cutie crowded in close, handing me one of the cold bottles, and I willingly pressed against him as he curled his free arm around my waist. Our mouths fused, and I pressed against his hard cock digging into my belly.

My head floated with a more than decent buzz, and even though he wasn't the greatest kisser in the world, my body hopped aboard the "let's fuck" train, growing all warm inside.

He palmed my ass as his lips trailed to my ear. "I want you," he said into my ear, and I wiggled in his grasp, moaning agreement even though he wouldn't hear above the music.

"Shaun!"

Krystal's shriek jerked my eyelids open. She focused on the door we'd entered through, and I pulled back enough from my lay of the night to get a better look through the crowd.

Dad.

"Oh, *fuck*!" The blood drained from my face, and I jerked out of my holder's arms completely, yanking my skirt back into place, suddenly wishing the damn thing was a good foot longer.

Dad had found me, and although he hadn't yet made eye contact with me while scanning the lounge, I knew there was no slipping away without notice. He was going to fucking kill me for giving my bodyguards the slip—or at least take my credit cards and car away for a while.

"Goddamnit!" Adrenaline coursed through my body, shaking my legs and hands, urging me to run, but I knew better.

Freedom ... gone. Better to face the damn music and get it over with.

I grabbed Krystal's hand and started toward Dad rather than the front door to make an attempted escape. Without a doubt, he had his goons surrounding the damn place anyway.

I caught a glimpse of his rumpled suit and loosened tie—neither of which he ever allowed in public —as Krystal and I jostled through the crowd.

What the...

Dad turned our way, and our gazes collided, his wide eyes full of an emotion I hadn't seen since I was ten—fear.

My breath caught, my stomach cramping, and I forced my feet to move faster, stumbling in my heels, desperate to get to him as I fought to keep my buzzed head focused.

Shaun, I saw his mouth move, but couldn't hear past the thumping music. Lips in a thin line, he hurried toward us, scanning the room, and my chest tightened, an ache growing in the back of my throat as desperation to reach him rolled over me.

"Dad!" I half sobbed the second he grabbed my upper arms and leaned in close without holding me like I'd hoped—without giving me the comfort I needed.

"We have to get out of here!" he said in my ear, and I didn't have a chance to respond before he yanked me toward the doorway leading to the office area.

My fingers ripped from Krystal's, but I didn't look back as fear and chills raced over my skin, bringing flashes of memories I'd attempted to bury over the past decade.

Mom in our kidnapper's hold.

Dad's screams.

Gunshots.

Another sob caught in my throat as Dad approached Buddy, who held the door open for us.

"Where's Krystal?" Buddy hollered as we rushed into the hallway.

I glanced over my shoulder, pointing but quickly jerked back around to keep from tripping after Dad, who held my other hand in a vise grip.

The door slammed shut behind us, my ears ringing at the loss of thumping music. Without a word, we sprinted down the hallway, my heels catching more than twice.

"Arturo," Dad finally said the second time I almost face-planted, his voice loud over the muffled thumps of bass emanating from the club.

One word—and the entire world as I'd known it, my life, screeched to a crashing halt.

Arturo.

The memory of dark eyes and black hair slicked into a ponytail flitted through my mind. He'd called me princess the handful of times he'd come to our house before Mom's death, and even then, I knew the man was evil as the devil himself.

"Did he get to my bodyguards?" I asked as we bypassed Buddy's office without stopping for my coat and purse.

"I don't know," Dad replied, his voice low and shaky. "But I'm not taking any chances."

His hair being mussed to hell was another no-no, and I quickly glanced down over his wrinkled suit coat to the askew hem caught up in the pistol shoved in his waistband. It wasn't the first I'd seen him carry, and with my dad's lifestyle, I knew it wouldn't be the last.

A smear of blood lay along the side of his neck. Even though a peace of sorts had been reached between Arturo and Dad, unrest had run rampant in our house the ten years since Mom's death.

"Are you injured?" My whisper sounded loud in my ears.

"No." He clipped the word and pulled up abruptly at the exit, turning to face me. He clasped my shoulders, and I peered up into his hazel eyes, fighting off the thickness in my throat at the emotions in his eyes that he usually held under tight rein. "He tried once before and took Joanna from me—he isn't going to take you, too."

A keening sounded deep in my throat, and Dad's lips thinned. "I need you to be strong, Shaun."

Trembling in his grasp, I fought like hell to keep hold of myself as the past crashed against me from all sides. I'd been ten and innocent, free from life's cares, ignorant of Dad being a kingpin, and the men who hated him.

"We have to go." Dad tugged me toward the exit once more even though I hadn't got anywhere near hold of myself as I'd have liked. "Stick to my heels—don't look at anyone, don't speak to anyone."

I nodded dumbly, using my free hand to swipe tears from my cheeks in an attempt to be the strong woman he wanted. If only he'd have offered a quick hug—the thing I always longed for and never received—the fortifying sense of having firm ground to stand upon, to *depend* upon outside of monetary means.

"The car's at the end of the alleyway. You'll get in the back, lay down, and stay down until I say."

I nodded again, knowing to never argue with Dad's commands.

One last quick scan of my face and he turned, grasping the exit door's handle. Dad peeked out head moving left then right. "Stay close," he whispered, pulling the door open far enough for us to slip through.

I stepped out into the dark after him, my breath loud in my ears as cold bit at my exposed, over-heated skin. Dad's dress shoes slapped on the sidewalk, my heels clicking as we hurried up the alleyway.

A crowd still stood at the front of the club, but Dad pushed through, people closing back in behind us as we fought to get to the car.

I kept my focus on his tense shoulders rather than scan the crowd for faces I might recognize—my guards, or his men from the compound I'd called home. Every muscle inside me trembled, shaking my limbs. The second we escaped the throng, he headed toward a tan car I didn't recognize, his head in constant motion as he scanned the immediate area.

Dad grasped the car's back door handle.

Pop!

"Get in!" he shouted as people began screaming behind us.

He yanked open the door, and I dove in headfirst, my heart in my throat.

Oh fuck, oh fuck, oh fuck...

I curled up on the cloth seat, hugging my knees to my chest, trembling from fear as much as the cold.

Another gunshot sounded, and Dad slammed the door behind me.

Please be okay... I clenched my eyelids shut.

A third shot sounded through the ringing in my ears, and I bit my lip to keep from shrieking, curling even tighter into myself. Tears rolled down my cheeks, and I held my breath ... waiting. Needing Dad to be okay. Needing him to get in the car and take me far away from the shit.

The driver door tore open, and a quick peek revealed Dad hopping in.

"Fuck!" He pulled away from the curb like a bat out of hell, tires squealing beneath us, and I clenched my eyes shut again, trying to still my breathing and calm the fuck down. Rather than spew a million questions and distract Dad as he muttered curses and sped down one road after another, I kept quiet except for sniffles when my nose threatened to drip.

Violence came with Dad's line of business. I'd learned that first hand, and the aftermath of that war had left me without a mother, left my father broken and shut down toward his only living relative—me.

The only daughter.

The only heir to the fortune and empire he'd built from running drugs with a cartel I wished I didn't know anything about.

"Shaun!" Dad barked. "Get your seat belt on. Now."

He swerved, and a car sped alongside us as I sat up. Two men sat in the front, neither of which I recognized.

The one in the passenger seat raised a gun.

"Gun!" I shrieked, and Dad slammed on the brakes.

Lower lip between my teeth, I slid out of the shoulder strap and laid back down, curling up as tight as I could.

Dad stomped on the gas again.

Metal scraped—the car shifted.

Dad cursed low and long...

We sped up. He slammed the brakes again enough to tumble me off the seat had I not had the belt across my lap. More speed, more metal screeching—tears and snot mingled on my face, but I couldn't be bothered to care.

I'd always thought keeping my eyes closed as a child meant no one could see me, that I hid in my own little world. Untouchable. Invincible.

I'd learned the day Mom died, the closing of one's eyes couldn't shield one from the horrors in life.

The car suddenly shifted—spun.

I bit my lip, tasting blood as I whimpered.

Sounds of screeching—metal smashing—a loud explosion.

Our car came to a standstill, silence engulfing the air around us.

I peeked to find Dad's face illuminated by bright, flashing light. He stared for all of two seconds before stomping on the gas and yanking the steering wheel.

Breath held, I watched him drive us away from whatever had happened, his head turning, non-stop scanning whatever lay around us. He let out a heavy exhale, and I did the same, knowing the threat of whoever had tried to run us off the road no longer pursued us.

My bladder somehow managed to hold onto the liquor I'd drunk while dancing my free night away. It twinged with discomfort, but I had bigger issues to focus on.

My old life is gone; I knew with us on the run. Not that I'd ever had plans of continuing the business Dad had begun as a teenager when he found out he would become a father at age sixteen. Already broke and living on the streets, he had no family to turn to and had chosen a path that would provide for his small family.

A horrible choice, one that shattered and broke other families, but he'd claimed it was just business.

I knew Dad had secreted money away over the years, so we wouldn't go without, but the thought of where we would go gnawed at my mind. In hiding, of that, I had no doubt. If he couldn't trust his men, he couldn't trust the two pilots that had spirited us around the country. He couldn't trust the captain of his yacht sitting in Boston's harbor.

He had no other family to hide us. My mother's parents had shunned my father after her death, and in retaliation, he'd kept me from seeing them. Not that I'd ever minded—they always used to put Dad down and talk shit about him to my face.

He might be a stern prick at times, pushed off my

attempts for affection until I learned to leave him alone, but he was still my daddy.

"You okay?" he finally asked after a good fifteen minutes of stifling quietness.

"Yes."

"Sit up and fix your seatbelt."

I made myself as small as possible in the corner of the backseat while taking note of the towering Hilltop sign glowing in Saugus's lights as we sped up Route 1. "Where are we going?"

"Topsfield."

My eyebrows pulled together. "What the hell is in Topsfield?"

"The Vicious Vipers, and watch your language."

I blinked, processing. I didn't know Dad had connections with the biker gang, but if the rumors I'd heard about the Vipers were true, we would at least be safely tucked away where no one would attempt to get their hands on us. The Vipers held a violent reputation, one built from long before I'd been born, before Dad, even. No one messed with them, not even the law.

Messing with one, or anyone under their protection, meant a quiet disappearance of the idiot who thought himself untouchable and an unsolved case that would be boxed up and forgotten.

My breath finally evened out, and I slumped against the seat, my head still floating from my buzz, the massive adrenaline rush leaving me depleted of energy.

"How'd you know where to find me tonight, Dad?"

"I have my connections."

I sighed. His usual answer kept me in the dark, but even though I loved having the money his business provided, I didn't want to *know* the business.

Fifteen minutes later, we approached a gated driveway, its fence reaching away on both sides until disappearing into the dark. A compound—more or less a cage to keep us safe.

Dad hated to be confined.

"You're going to leave me here, aren't you?" I asked as that truth slipped through my brain.

"Yes."

"And where are *you* going?" I asked, a ripple of unease causing goosebumps to break out across my skin.

Dad put the car into park and returned both hands to the steering wheel as a bulk of a man approached from the guardhouse. "To end this once and for all."

That tone meant nothing would stop him from

doing what he planned, so I didn't even bother trying, even though the thought of his going after Arturo churned my stomach.

"You'd better return to get me," I whispered as the hulking man cut off the floodlight atop the guardhouse and tapped on the driver window.

Dad lowered the window rather than respond to me, and a heavy shadow slipped through my thoughts, tightening my chest once more.

2

DREW

A sense of foreboding hovered over my mind long into the evening, regardless of the party kicking at the club. I'd dreamed about her again, and even though I couldn't clearly recall her face, her presence had haunted my head all goddamn day.

Disturbed screamed through the new Bose system Vigil, our president, had installed in the lounge area of our club, but no one seemed to be listening. Brothers played cards, shot pool, and slammed back shots while the club girls sat on their laps or knelt between thighs, swallowing down Viper dicks easy as water.

I sat at the bar's end with a tonic, keeping an eye on everyone and everything. I'd earned the nickname Warden while prospecting since I felt responsible for damn near every friend I made—and the fact I ran a bodyguard service outside of the club during normal work hours.

The sense of ... something ... kept me from sucking down a beer while one of the girls sucked on me. I felt the need to be on top of my game, alert, and ready for shit. Since the only other brother probably not getting drunk off his ass sat guard at the front gate, I felt it my duty as a Viper enforcer to watch over my brothers.

Ryker, our Sergeant at Arms, and one mean son of a bitch who liked his real goddamn name, thank you very much, caught my eye from across the room, his cell pressed to his ear. His mouth moved while speaking to whoever was on the line. Seconds later, he stood and made his way toward me, shoving his cell in his back pocket, lips flat-lined.

"What's up?" I asked when he got close enough to hear me over the music.

"Stone called. Said there's someone at the gate asking for you."

I frowned same as Ryker and glanced at the club's door as though I might see through the metal. "He say who it is?"

"Ben Thode."

"Fucking hell," I grumbled beneath my breath, the dream of his wife rushing through my damn brain again with an intensity that knifed at my gut. "Fuck," I cursed again, pushed my tonic aside, and started toward the door, Ryker on my heels.

"Why the fuck is the goddamn cartel's kingpin here and asking for you, Warden?"

I yanked the door open but didn't turn to answer while stepping out into the cold night in my white t-shirt and leather cut. "We have history."

"Good, bad, or ugly?"

"All fucking three."

My breath fogged as I strode across the drive toward the compound's entrance, ready for the trouble I'd been anticipating all day, tension heated my blood, keeping me way too fucking warm.

Ben Thode. Childhood best friend, the brother I'd never had. The man I'd given up my teenage crush for. He'd gotten the girl, then got her pregnant when we were all sixteen. Last I'd seen him had been the morning his wife and daughter had been kidnapped, the same day Joanna died—because I hadn't been there to protect her as I'd been hired to do. Assuming my position as a bodyguard had been ended by my pissed off friend, I'd stayed away. Selfishness—the desire to live—had kept me from attending the funeral and nearing the Thode compound ever again.

I had expected to be taken out for my failure, but the minutes, the days had passed without a single threat on my life.

It'd been ten fucking years since I'd seen him.

And the guilt still festered even if my own grief over Joanna's death had faded a bit. But the dreams...

I fisted my hands to keep them from shaking. Focus honed in on the idling car beyond the gate and the headlights keeping me from seeing beyond their glare, I approached with caution even though I knew Stone would have made sure Ben wasn't packing.

Ryker and I stopped a few feet from the gate, and I nodded at Stone in the guardhouse. Seconds later, a buzzer sounded, and the gate began shifting toward the right, the racket of metal rollers screeching in my head.

I fought to keep my breathing even while eyeing the beat up, light sedan as it pulled into the compound and stopped alongside me. The lowered driver window gave me a glimpse of the man I'd loved like a brother once upon a time.

"Ben."

Lips pursed, he finally looked up at me, resignation, fear, and a whole other slew of emotions I couldn't catch flitting over his face before he shut them down into the mask he'd created since becoming a big man in the drug world.

He climbed out of the car but kept his distance. "Drew," he said, his voice low, as though unsure of himself, something he never used to be.

I nodded, quietly taking note of his rumpled designer suit, the scuffed leather dress shoes, the askew tie, and dark smear of what looked like blood on his neck. For him to show up at the Vipers compound, a far cry from his usual put-together self...

"What are you doing here?" I asked, the hairs on the nape of my neck stirring.

The car's back door opened, and long legs—bare to the thigh where a black leather skirt hugged tanned skin—slipped out into view. She stood in expensive heels, her bared stomach flat and taut, gorgeous tits smooshed into a halter top that threatened to spill the goods.

Her arms wrapped around her waist against the cold, and I lifted my gaze to her face.

Joanna.

I stared, dumbstruck, the air in my lungs strangled the fuck right off as our gazes collided.

"*Him?*" she whispered with venom enough to kill a man while shooting a glare at Ben. "You've got to be fucking *kidding* me!"

"Shaun," Ben snipped, "language."

Shaun—his daughter. Joanna's daughter. I stared.

"Why him?" she all but spit as I struggled to find my voice. "He failed you once before and you—"

"Calm down, Shaun."

"Calm down?" she hollered, hands fisting at her sides as my attention flitted back and forth between the two of them. "It's *his* fault—"

"I don't have any other choice!" Ben's shout clamped her lips shut, but she glared at him while letting a huff out of her nose and crossing her arms again.

He let out a heavy sigh, his head hanging. "I know you hate him—"

"Understatement of the year, "she muttered, shooting daggers at me with her eyes.

"—but I *know* Drew, Shaun. He's the only man I know right now that can't be bought. He's loyal."

"Yeah, well, he wasn't very loyal to you back in the day," she said, her lip curling as she took me in from head to toe.

"That's the past," Ben said, his voice still quiet. "And neither of us is the man we were back then."

"Care to tell us what the *fuck* is going on?" Ryker asked, putting an end to their argument as I tore my attention off eyes as blue as a jay's feathers.

Ben kept his focus on my face, and I knew what he planned on asking before he even opened his damn mouth. "I need you to protect her."

I swallowed, my goddamn heart thundering in my ears. I'd dreamed of a second chance to prove myself to him, but... "Ben—"

"Please, Drew," the fucker cut me off. "You're the only one I can trust."

Shaun snorted.

"What happened?" I asked, ignoring her look of death as my brain came back online, computing the truth of that *something* I'd been feeling all goddamn day.

"Arturo infiltrated my compound—quietly and thoroughly, buying off my men. I'm lucky I escaped."

I motioned toward my neck in the same spot blood smeared along his. "You injured?"

"Just a scratch."

"The men at your place?"

"I had to shoot my way out," he said with a shrug, zero trace of remorse in his voice.

"Oh, Daddy." Shaun's voice broke as though just learning that information herself, but she didn't go to him, didn't offer support. Just stood there, hugging herself.

If Ben shot his way out, bodies littered his house and grounds. I had no doubt. The man knew how to handle a gun and seemed unmoved from having to take out some of his own men. He'd been on the path to becoming a cold-hearted bastard last I'd seen him. I guessed losing Joanna had tipped him off that goddamn iceberg.

"Whose car?" I asked, eyeing the piece of shit.

"Stolen, and I tossed my cell—there's no way we were traced here."

I nodded, although my gut still twisted.

"Shaun's cell?" I asked.

"Left behind," she sniped. "Just like the rest of my goddamn life."

"Shaun!"

"Sorry, Dad," she muttered, glancing away, her shoulders finally wilting.

"I blamed you for so long, Drew," Ben said, his

voice low as he turned his attention back on me. "No one will believe I brought her here—to you."

He spoke truth. Arturo's men wouldn't look for Shaun if she hid with the Vipers. Even if he did find out where Ben hid her, the fucker knew better than to come after a person under our protection—*if* Vigil would offer it to Ben and his daughter.

Still, I hesitated from agreeing as a slew of emotions continued to ransack my brain, guilt holding the lead over dread, and the fear it might start a war I knew Vigil wouldn't want.

"You owe me." Ben's whispered words knifed my chest.

Penance for my sins. I closed my eyes. *Final nail in the fucking coffin.*

I inhaled until it hurt, and glanced over at Ryker, raising an eyebrow in silent question.

"Bring them in back," he said. "I'll open Vigil's office door. We can talk more there." He turned toward Ben. "You packing?"

"Glock's right here," Stone said, moving toward us to hand the gun over to Ryker.

He took the piece, shoved it behind his waistband, and nodded his head toward Ben. "Warden."

I knew what Ryker asked, but my heart beat

heavy as I approached Ben. "Arms out," I said, my voice gruffer than necessary.

I patted him down, wanting to hug rather than frisk while Ryker did a quick search of the car. I'd missed the fucker, hated that I'd been the reason Joanna no longer breathed and hated that I'd lost my best friend that day, too.

"Pull around the right of the main building there," I told Ben once I finished, motioning at the club's main building behind us.

Ben nodded and turned toward Shaun. She glared at me, eyes narrowed in a kill stare.

"What?" she spit at me. "Don't have the balls to pat me down, too?"

I grinned, although no amusement induced my lips upward. She remembered me for what I'd *not* done—protect her and her mother—but I wondered if she remembered the man I'd been before that day. Rides on my shoulders. Tea parties with her dolls since her dad didn't allow play dates. Walks at the beach. Countless hours at the park on swings... I'd been her big teddy bear.

Gone. All in a blink because of my goddamn self-ishness.

And Shaun was no longer a little girl. That was for damn sure, but I needed to put my brain—and her attitude—in check if she was going to be hanging around the Vipers' compound.

Unable to help myself, I glanced down over her gorgeous, too-young body. "Sweetheart, if you're packing beneath that tight ass skirt and top, squeezing the life out of your tits—"

"I'll do it," Ryker said, but I shot out my hand in a sudden surge of anger and grasped his arm to stop his forward momentum.

"You don't touch her." My words came out with a threatening tone, straight the fuck up possessive as hell.

Instant tension flared to life between Ryker and me, but Ben chuckled. "And *that* is why I brought you to Drew, Shaun."

Drew. Ben didn't know the man I'd become, the warden with a dozen kills to my name, and a reputation for violence when needed.

I took a step forward as though to frisk her myself, but she yelped and scrambled back into the car, losing one heel and flashing white panties between her thighs in the process.

Goddamn.

The door slammed shut behind her, and I turned, teeth clenched against my dick's sudden interest in the last woman I should lust after.

Ben climbed in the driver's side but caught my eye. "I trust you to protect her, Drew, but if you or anyone of these bastards so much as lay one goddamn finger on her—"

"Pull the piece of shit car around back, Ben," I cut him short, my usual tolerance for bullshit at zero. "You know I'd give you the skin off my back if you asked. That's never changed. Never will." I strode away, my shoulders tense as fuck, my head a goddamn kaleidoscope of emotion I didn't know how to sort.

My best friend and his hot as fuck, leggy daughter who looked almost identical to my first love had crashed into my life.

What the fuck had fate slapped onto my plate? Or, had karma come knocking for her due for the life I'd chosen to live? Either one, I knew it wasn't going to be pretty ... or end well.

———

"No fucking way, Dad," Shaun said for at least the fifth time since we'd gotten to Vigil's office. She sat with her legs tucked beneath her on a couch that had probably seen more action than my favorite boots I wore just about every damn day.

We all ignored her, same as the other times she grumbled about her father's plan to leave her behind.

Ryker stood by the door leading into the club room beyond, arms crossed, anger still lining his face with deep grooves. I expected we'd have words over my touching his arm—the man hated when people touched him without permission.

I'd do it all over again. I wasn't about to let anyone paw at Shaun since she was Ben's daughter—not because my dick wanted her all to myself.

That's what I told myself, anyway.

I let out a slow exhale, focusing on Ben seated beside her, his gaze piercing—and pleading.

"With Shaun safe here, I can focus on finishing what I've been working on for ten years," he said. "I know I can get in and take Arturo out before he knows I'm there."

I lifted an eyebrow. "How the fuck you gonna do that? You go all ninja shit or something since I saw you last?"

Ben sat back, a darkness in his eyes I'd never seen before. He'd been hardened by a shitty life, that much was evident, even if he had the cash to burn and properties all over the fucking planet. "A lot has changed since Joanna's death."

I didn't glance at Shaun as agreement he spoke the truth shot through my brain. I didn't know the Ben with the lines on his face and a few gray hairs above his temple—same as he didn't know me. His daughter had been a little kid, one with evidence of eventual beauty, but the body, those curves that had sprung to life in the time since I'd seen her last...

I clenched my jaw against my wandering thoughts. "She stays here with my brothers, and I'm going with you to finish this," I said through my teeth, not sure I'd be able to keep my own damn paws off her.

"No," he muttered at the same time Shaun huffed a, "Yes, *please*."

She continued muttering about me being an asshole and her not wanting to look at my ugly mug every day until her dad got back.

I held Ben's stare, ignoring the sassy brat who needed to have her spoiled ass spanked as her father reminded her of her language.

"Can't let you go alone," I told him. "You might have the intel, the floor plans to his place near the city, but it's a suicide mission. He's probably scouring the entire east coast for you and has his own place on lockdown. What the fuck makes you think you'll get inside his ten-foot walls, past dozens of guards?"

Ben's eyes gleamed, remnants of childhood mischievousness mingling with the darkness pooling in their depths. "Arturo and I agreed to a truce all those years ago, but we're both patient men. I've been planning my retribution for Joanna's death since the day his cousin took her, Drew. He had people in my house, but I have mine in his."

"Who?"

His lips quirked and flatlined again. "His wife, for one."

"What?" Shaun whispered with fierce pissiness, scrambling to sit up.

Ben ignored her, as did I while I stewed over that tidbit of information. Shaun's reaction to the news he had a woman in his life made me think Ben hadn't ever moved on from Joanna.

"How long you been fucking her?" I asked.

"Almost five years."

"What the *fuck*, Dad?" Shaun whispered harshly, hurt evident in her voice.

"Language, Shaun!"

"How could you betray—"

"Shaun!" Ben glanced at her, his eyes cold. "Enough!"

She crossed her arms with a huff, but I caught the sheen of tears in her eyes—and the fact she seemed to hug herself rather than sulk. I wondered over the last time she'd been shown affection. God knew it hadn't ever come naturally for Ben, and he'd never let her have a real friend.

"You're sure about this?" I asked, turning toward him.

"Dead."

I grimaced at Ben's word choice, but dipped my head once in agreement, knowing the stubborn fucker wouldn't be talked out of it.

Some of the tension left his shoulders, but his stare didn't lighten. "Thank you, brother."

My goddamn throat threatened to swell. I'd gotten my best friend back, but I'd also gained a thorn in my side, who given the chance, would probably try to bury a knife in my back.

I turned my focus on Shaun and instantly regretted doing so. Fire in her wet eyes singed me—and twitched my dick to life again. Jaw clenched, I reminded myself she was just a kid, and that I'd *fucked her mom*, even if it only was the one time. Never mind, I'd been the one responsible for her death.

Dick put in its place, limp and hanging to the left, I stood and held out my hand to Ben.

He jolted upward to take my hand, pulling me in

for a half-hug, thumping my back three times as we'd always used to greet one another.

"Fucking twilight zone," Shaun muttered from where she once more glaring from the couch.

I couldn't have agreed more.

3
___

SHAUN

Sure, Dad hugged the man responsible for Mom's death rather than his only daughter, who felt like the ground beneath her had been blown to chunks of unstable bullshit.

My eyes stung at the insult, and I made myself small on the couch, hugging myself tighter. Nothing like the affection I starved for, given to a mere stranger to worsen my buzzed pissiness.

Dad had an in with the biker gang, which would ensure my safety, but my hatred of the man he would leave me with did *not* sit well in my head and churning stomach. I would prefer to make Drew's life a living hell, but for the sake of my father, I would attempt to stifle my anger.

I would agree to stay since Dad trusted Drew and

his Viper brothers, but I would always hate him. He was what kept *me* from being the guilty one.

Pushing aside that sickening thought, I focused on the man Dad slapped on the back.

Drew, or Warden as his biker brothers called him, stood a few inches taller than Dad, dark, almond-shaped eyes, and his skin sun-kissed with just enough natural tan I wondered at his heritage. Black hair, full black beard—both held evidence of age, but I found the few grays and the lines crinkling at the sides of his eyes sexy as hell.

Telling myself I wasn't even remotely attracted to his hot ass, he was *Dad's age* for fuck's sake, my gaze quickly roamed down his body. I loved the full sleeve tattoos covering his muscular, veiny arms, the trim waist, and the powerful looking thighs filling out his worn jeans. Old boots encased his feet, and my lips actually twitched to smirk at the thought he was such an ass that the damn things must be his best friends since losing Dad.

My gaze flew upward as Dad pulled away from their hug, and my focus abruptly snagged on the bulge in Drew's jeans.

Good God, almighty...

My mouth watered, and I scowled, squeezing my thighs together. Heat swarmed through me as his dark-eyed gaze collided with mine. The smoothest chocolate orbs, promising to satisfy...

What. The. Fuck.

Scowling even deeper, I lifted my chin and flitted my still alcohol-slowed focus around the room, hoping he caught my *I hate you* vibe I wanted to stay anchored in my soul.

Ryker stood by the door, his stare steady on my face, and I shifted on the couch, glancing down at my arms wrapped around my middle. He seemed like one nasty, mean bastard, one who'd been more than willing to get his hands on me.

I'd wanted to get laid earlier that night, but no, thank you, Mr. Ryker.

A bunch of other horny bikers probably partied beyond the door he guarded. Younger, I thought, my mind flitting about in alcohol remnants even though exhaustion sank me into the filthy couch. Men more my type.

Perhaps hanging with the Vipers wouldn't be so bad. No PITAs to make men ignore me like they'd been famous for.

"Will you stay the night?" Drew asked my dad, pulling me back to the Vipers' office.

"Arturo will expect me to run with my daughter,

probably to our villa in Italy, so I'm going to take advantage of that."

Drew nodded, eyeing dad's outfit once more. "What do you need? Clothes? Guns? Name it we got it."

"Seeing as how my men he'd swayed knew of my safe house, I've got nothing local. I'll take whatever you can get me," Dad said. "And that piece of shit car—Arturo's men put up a chase for close to a mile. Didn't end well for them, but if you've got some sort of wheels to get me back into Boston?"

Drew clasped his shoulder, glanced at me quickly, then at Ryker. "Hang here while I get Drew set up?"

Ryker nodded, his lips in a thin line, his eyes like a shark's.

I shivered and curled in on myself, resting my head on the couch's arm, uncaring of the filth ground into its scratchy material.

Dad and Drew disappeared through the door into the club with a blast of music from beyond, and the second the door slammed shut, I expelled a heavy sigh. Coming to terms with my immediate future, I forced my entire body to relax. The excitement, flight up Route 1, being bombarded with a shit load of unwanted emotions, took their toll on me, never mind too much alcohol, and I closed my eyes.

—————

Drew smelled fine as fuck. Like, tingle between the thighs and get wet for cock, kind of luscious scent. All woodsy with hints of musk and citrus.

Still scowling, I leaned against the passenger door of his truck, trying to get as far away from him as possible while we drove in silence.

There was no room for us at the inn—or rather, Drew hadn't been about to keep me on the Viper's compound surrounded by a bunch of horny bikers.

I must be ovulating or some such shit. I heaved a sigh and rested my forehead on the passenger window, trying to focus on the cold rather than the lingering need to get laid. I'd only been able to sneak two guys in three years into my room while at college, and it'd been over eight months since the last one.

Even finally having our own apartment hadn't ensured any type of freedom, thanks to my shadows who stuck to me like stink on a skunk's ass.

Those three boys had been lucky to make it in and out—pun intended—because if my babysitters had seen them, had known what we'd done, those boys would have ended up swimming with the fishes deep in the Atlantic, never to be seen or heard from again.

Dating, like cursing, was frowned upon by Dad.

Fucking twenty, and I hadn't been allowed off on my own, hadn't been able to escape. Yes, I'd tried. A handful of times after turning eighteen, but Dad must have implanted a damn tracking device on me or something.

Damn connections.

Rarely did I nab freedom for longer than two hours before being found.

And, I found out he'd been fucking around with Arturo's wife for almost five years. I huffed a snort over Dad forgetting about Mom in such a way—and with his number one enemy's wife? I was starting to think I didn't know my father as well as I'd thought I did.

He hadn't hugged me goodbye, merely nodded at me from a distance while I stood, arms wrapped around my torso, giving myself the comfort I desperately craved—needed—from him at that moment.

Come back for me, I'd whispered in my head, but he'd turned without a word, climbed into the car he'd been gifted—with the old smashed up sedan's plates—and drove out of the Viper's compound into the night, leaving me behind.

With a hot as fuck asshole who ought to be six feet under in my mom's place.

Emotional exhaustion pulled on my eyelids even though I'd caught a cat nap while in the office that smelled like beer and cigarettes.

"Just a couple more minutes," Drew said, but I ignored him. "I don't have a guest bed, so you can have mine. I'll sleep on the couch."

Such an offer deserved a thank you, but he wasn't going to get jack from me.

He let out a shallow sigh. "You look just like Joanna." His voice was quiet as though lost in the past—one I remembered all too well and wished I didn't.

I pretended to not hear his murmur, since I wasn't about to thank him like I'd done countless others for that compliment over the years. Mom had been beautiful. The pictures I kept in my room never allowed me to forget her.

As Dad seemed to have done.

We snaked our way up a winding hill, trees blotting out any view but the black sky above. Deep in the woods, sudden motion flood lights filled my vision, and I blinked, taking a quick look at the small cabin in the clearing.

Homey and tidy. A bachelor's pad tucked away deep in the forest where no one might find us... All alone. My pussy twinged with interest, and I scowled again.

Damn it, body!

Drew pulled into a garage, and the engine shut off, leaving us in silence. He let out a loud exhale before climbing out of the truck. Resigned—but still pissy—I did the same and stepped past his delicious smelling body when he motioned me through the door and into the house.

Small kitchen. Small living area beyond. Fireplace and leather couch.

The whole damn place smelled like him, so I opted for tiny breaths, keeping as much of his arousing scent out of my nose as I could.

I moved farther into the open-plan area, noting stairs leading up on the right.

"Bedroom is up there," Drew said, his keys clinking as he tossed them onto the counter. "Bathroom, too."

Not bothering to acknowledge him, I kicked off my Jimmy Choos, leaving them where they lay at the foot of the stairs, and trudged upward.

Two rooms, one with a bed, the other an office. Bathroom.

Score. I locked the door behind me and took care of business since I hadn't been about to touch a bathroom at the Vipers' club. God knew what sort of fun stuff I'd see in there.

"If you want to take a shower, towels are under the sink," Drew said through the door. "I'll grab you something to wear."

A shower sounded like heaven, and I turned on the sprayer, hoping to wash away the shit show from the previous couple of hours.

Before pulling my top off, I glanced at the bathroom's ceiling, checking for cameras like Dad kept throughout our massive house I'd been happy to leave—once upon a time.

My throat swelled, but I pushed aside morbid thoughts of never getting to go home again. For so long, I'd wanted to escape, but having found that freedom in an off the wall sort of way, I'd have given anything in that moment to be back under Dad's roof in my own bathroom.

Not seeing any cameras, I stripped, tied my hair up in a knot the best I could, and climbed beneath the hot spray, determined to stay strong even as my eyes welled.

Tears escaped, and I allowed them, surprised with myself for having held them in for so long, since the past had rushed to swamp my mind the second I'd laid eyes on Drew.

It had been ten years, and while I remembered well his laughing brown eyes and easy smile, I'd known him as a child—me innocent and carefree, him like a favorite uncle since I didn't have a real one. That had changed the day Mom died, the day he hadn't done the job Dad had hired him to do.

Protect us. Keep us safe.

Chin tilting up, I grabbed his bar of soap and made quick work of washing the dried sweat and fear off my body, even as his scent flooded the steamed shower and the suds caressing down my body drained away.

Five minutes later, I yanked open the bathroom door, a large gray towel tucked between my breasts and falling mid-thigh, expecting to see my newest babysitter.

No Drew.

I tiptoed to the bedroom door and noted a t-shirt at the bed's foot that hadn't been there when I'd passed the doorway the first time.

"Damnit," I muttered while pulling the shirt down over my head. The damn thing seemed steeped in Drew's scent. Soap, laundry detergent, cologne—whatever it was, or even all three combined, pressed my thighs together with needy friction.

I shoved my arms through the too-large holes as the shirt settled down over me, and I finally released the towel from its hold over my breasts.

Too damn exhausted to give a fuck, I stole his bed—he deserved it, anyway—I climbed between the covers and burrowed into a pillow that also smothered me in his hot as fuck aroma. I'd been gifted an opportunity to make Drew Tellier pay for my mother's death, and I would make that my focus until Dad came to get me.

Eyes closing, I breathed in a warm scent I wanted to hate while wracking my brain for a plan, but sleep claimed me before any brilliant ideas popped into my mind.

4

DREW

I couldn't fucking sleep and became well acquainted with my living room's ceiling barely visible from the nightlight I kept on in the kitchen. Living in the sticks meant no outside light. It meant pitch black during a new moon, which had begun its descent hours earlier.

Anger over having Ben take off on his own warred with my balls' need to empty. It'd been too damn long since I'd had one of the club girls, and the fuckers between my legs ached thanks to the young woman sleeping in my bed.

I'd left out a shirt for her, and twenty or so minutes after the shower shutting off and her not coming downstairs, I'd gone up to check on her.

Shaun had passed out, hugging my pillow, her

dark hair spilled across my sheets, her plump lips parted in sleep. So much like Joanna—and yet not, with a fiery spirit and sassy mouth all her own. Beautiful as fuck, alluring as a mythical creature, and just like her mother, not meant for me.

My dick didn't give a fuck and stiffened in my sweatpants anyway.

Jaw clenching for the hundredth time that night, I tossed my forearm over my eyes, fighting off the want, tightening my balls again.

"Jesus Christ," I muttered, and grabbed my dick, because why the hell not? I told myself I wasn't jerking off to the thought of Joanna's daughter. Ben's daughter.

A few, hard strokes, and cum shot up onto my abs, and I grunted, hips thrusting until my balls emptied. I chose to live in denial that it'd been Shaun's face flashing through my mind while coming and cleaned myself up with the t-shirt I'd ripped off before lying down on the couch.

Still staring at the ceiling, although a bit more relaxed, I prayed like hell Ben would take care of business and get his daughter out of my house quick as fuck.

Before I ended up eating her young pussy. Fucking every damn hole in her hot, tight body regardless of how much she hated me. I usually just took what I wanted, when I wanted, and my dick sure as hell wanted Shaun.

"Christ," I muttered again, and rolled onto my stomach, punching the second pillow I'd grabbed off my bed while she had been sleeping.

I wouldn't fuck his daughter. I wouldn't fuck a too-young girl that had grown to life in the belly of the first girl I'd ever had, the only woman I'd ever loved.

"Fucking sick," I told myself, but damn my dick for not agreeing.

———

I cracked open an eyelid and scowled as reality slammed into my brain.

A ward lay upstairs between my sheets all alone, probably all warm and soft.

Sexy and sassy as hell—and off-limits.

The sun crested the rise outside my cabin's front windows, and I considered the Saturday ahead to get my mind and morning wood off Shaun. Other than plans to hit the gym, I didn't have anything pressing to keep me distracted from the young woman I wanted to bury my dick inside.

The gym would be out since I couldn't take Shaun there and I couldn't leave her alone at my house. A goddamn thorn in my side—in more ways than one—until I heard from Ben.

Still scowling, I tossed off the throw blanket I'd pulled atop me during the night after the fire inside me finally subsided and stumbled into the kitchen.

Shaun would need clothes. Toiletries or whatever such shit women needed to get by for a day or two.

Hopefully, not any longer than that.

I turned on the coffee maker and stared at it while scratching my chest, wishing it would hurry the fuck up and fill the damn carafe. One of the club girls would get whatever I needed. After I got some coffee in my stomach and my brain plugged in, I would make a call.

A tingle lifted the hairs on the back of my neck, but I didn't turn.

Ears alert and senses suddenly awake, I listened to a brush of footfalls on the stairs, bringing the sassy brat into the living space much too small for the two of us.

"Coffee?" she questioned, her tone husky from sleep.

My semi took a liking to the siren's call of her

voice and stiffened, quick as fuck. "Brewing," I snipped.

"Cream and sugar?"

I yanked open the fridge door beside me and pulled out the milk. "Sugar's in the cabinet to the left of the stove," I grumbled, not about to turn around for Shaun to see my tented sweats.

The cabinet opened, and I glanced to my left for a quick peek.

Fuck.

Shaun stood on tiptoe, reaching for the sugar bag on the top shelf, lifting my shirt she'd worn to bed.

Fuck. Me. My head whispered again as I imagined her long legs wrapped around my head while I buried my face between the smooth thighs she showed off.

Did she show them off out of innocence or to taunt the ever-loving fuck outta me?

Teeth clenched, I forced my attention back on the coffee maker that began to sputter and cough up the last of the water in its reservoir.

"Have you heard from my dad yet?" Shaun asked, sitting at the table rather than sidling up to me to wait for her coffee.

"No."

She sighed. "Of all the people, why'd he have to leave me with you?" she grumbled, ticking a muscle in my jaw.

"I'm not too happy with the arrangement, either, sweetheart," I shot back, grumpy as fuck. Turned on as fuck.

The coffee pot beeped, and I yanked the carafe out, pouring into my waiting cup. I hadn't grabbed a mug for Shaun—and I hadn't bothered even after hearing she wanted some.

"Help yourself," I said, spinning away from the pot—*her*—and heading toward the stairs.

"Dick," she mumbled under her breath, probably at my lack of hospitality.

If only she knew that my dick led the way upstairs. I wondered if that sight would shut her damn mouth and make her appreciate her dad even had someone he could trust while shit went down. I had no doubt Arturo would have put a bullet in Ben's brain and taken Shaun for himself if given the chance. The fucker not only ran the goddamn drug ring in the entire New England area, but the Vipers had heard rumors he'd gotten into the skin market, too.

She ought to be grateful *she's under my protection instead.*

Temptation to turn around and give her an earful—and an eyeful of my dick—slowed my steps. Ben would kill me for scaring her like that, though. He'd always tried to protect her from the truth of his business.

I burned my tongue on my first big slug of coffee, and cursed, stomping upward.

Balls emptied in the shower, one cup of coffee in me, and a call for woman shit into the club, I returned downstairs in jeans and a t-shirt. Time to refill my cup and escape to my office to pretend to work so I wouldn't have to be around the spoiled bitch who'd been dumped on me.

She had every reason to hate me, but knowing that, and the fact I hated myself for her mother's death, didn't make my penance any easier.

Shaun had migrated to the couch, her knees drawn up to her chest inside my t-shirt, stretching the fucking thing out. Her hands wrapped around a steaming cup—her second, I assumed, while reaching for the carafe.

The fucking thing was empty.

"The fuck?" I muttered, shoving it back.

"Sorry, not sorry."

"Bitch," I grumbled and grabbed the coffee

container. "How the fuck did you drink the whole fucking pot in twenty goddamn minutes?"

"It's a small pot," she shot back, haughty and snippy as fuck.

My dick twitched, and I clenched my teeth while measuring out more grounds, unable to decide if I liked our shared hatred of mornings and love of coffee or not.

She stared out the window while I waited, hands on the counter, listening to the slow as fuck coffee pot do its job—again.

Second cup in hand, I strode into the living room, not wanting to be a gracious host, but having already made the call for necessities for my unwanted houseguest.

"One of the club girls is getting some things for you," I said, eyeing my shirt she'd ruined.

"Thank fuck," she muttered. "This t-shirt stinks."

"You're welcome to take it off." I shot back as she glared up at me. "Put back on your slutty outfit from last night—or run around naked."

"You'd like that, wouldn't you?"

I glanced down at what skin I could see, mainly her cute as fuck toes peeking from beneath my shirt's hem.

Fire burned in her eyes when I focused on her

face again, and I found myself grinning, enjoying our banter entirely too much. "I wouldn't complain, sweetheart."

She made a snorted, huffed sound and turned away from me, sipping her coffee.

I considered her—us—a few seconds before letting out a heavy exhale and taking a sip of hot as fuck black nectar. "Look, you hate me, I get that, but it is what it is, and until your dad gets back, you're stuck with me."

Her lips thinned. "Can I call my friend to let her know where I am? Dad dragged me away from her without an explanation—she's probably worried sick."

"No calls," I shot out without thought. "I'm not taking a single chance of anyone learning your whereabouts."

Shaun frowned.

"I've got work to do," I lied, "but Tina should be here within the hour. Maybe she'll hang, and you two can watch chick flicks or something to pass the time."

"No *fucking* thank you," she muttered.

"Language, Shaun," I couldn't help but shoot over my shoulder as I strode away. I made it halfway up the stairs before she spoke.

"How many times did you have that club whore —Tina, I think you called her?"

My lips twitched, and my palms itched to redden her ass. "Too many to count." Chuckling under my breath, I escaped upstairs. Shaun's arrival had stirred up memories I'd thought I'd dealt with, but the emotions she evoked in me—I couldn't decide if I wanted to throttle, choke, or fuck her brains out.

All three sounded fine as fuck.

5

———

SHAUN

The whore showed up an hour later, but I stayed put on Drew's couch at the knock, waiting for him to answer the door.

He hurried down the stairs without looking at me, and I turned away as though unaffected by his presence, the mere sight of his muscles, sexy tattoos, and beard I wanted to tug on while feasting on his lips.

I refused to acknowledge the jealousy slithering through my stomach while curling into a ball beneath a throw blanket he must have used the night before. It smelled divine, but I sure as hell didn't want him. Nope. The whore could have his sexy ass and that huge dick I'd noticed earlier that morning before he'd escaped upstairs for a long shower—where he'd probably jerked off, deep groans rumbling from his chest.

I shifted on the couch.

"Warden," a woman's voice purred when the door opened.

I rolled my eyes.

"Thanks for this, Tina," Drew said, the crinkling of plastic bags reaching me. "I owe you one."

"I wouldn't mind payment now," she told him with a throaty giggle, and I scowled, imagining her running a fingernail over his tight t-shirt and the pecs beneath.

"Later, Tina." His tone refused argument, and I smirked at her disappointed sigh.

A minute later, the door closed and Drew rounded the couch, bringing along his luscious scent.

"Here." He tossed the bags at my feet while I tried to squash my body's warm, wet reaction to his nearness. "Clothes and whatever else Tina thought you might need."

I nodded rather than offer thanks, and climbed off the couch, grasping the bags. Without a word, I scurried past him and upstairs, then locked myself in the bathroom.

The whore had brought me second-hand shit,

but at least it smelled clean and covered me better than Drew's shirt. I balled up the offensive cotton and tossed it into his hamper, hopeful I'd never have to wear anything of his again.

The clothes Tina had brought fit—mostly. My boobs spilled out of the sports bra she'd included, but it was better than nothing. Granny panties, leggings, long-sleeve t-shirt and sweatshirt all did their job, keeping me covered and warm.

A pair of flip flops sat at the bottom of one bag, and I rolled my eyes. No socks. No warm booties for the cold fall attacking New England. Damn flip flops, but better than my heels, I supposed.

Not that I'd be going anywhere.

At least the toothbrush Tina had tossed in was still in its packaging. No other toiletries, no womanly products—not that I needed them, anyway. My birth control shot kept Aunt Flo from making monthly visits, thank fuck.

I squeaked open the bathroom door and peered into the hallway. Noise sounded from the kitchen— fridge door and a pot clanging. If he was making lunch, I had a few seconds. I tiptoed toward his office, careful to keep my flip flops from giving away my destination with their tell-tale snap.

Knowing Krystal had to be freaking out—and

that I could trust her with my life—I slipped inside and shut the door quietly behind me. She knew who my dad was, who he did business with. She knew about the war that I'd thought ended with Mom's death, and she'd also gotten the truth of whose fault it had really been from me.

But blaming Drew came easier, and I'd never told another soul who was really responsible for that day's disastrous outcome.

A quick call on Drew's landline put me through to Krystal's voicemail—not that I'd expected her to answer the unknown number.

"Hey," I whispered after the beep, my heart pounding in my chest. "It's Shaun. I'm fine. Just wanted to let you know I probably won't be around for a few days, but don't worry—and don't call this number back. I'll get in touch with you as soon as I can. Love ya. Bye."

Once outside the office door again, I hesitated, my legs shaking from the adrenaline pumping through my blood. My stomach grumbled over the lack of food—Drew was *such* a gracious host—but I didn't want to be anywhere near him. I eyed the doorway leading into his bedroom.

Seeing as how I hadn't slept very well and I'd become about desperate to waste away the hours without my babysitter hovering, I decided on a nap.

Mistake.

I'd forgotten how much the bed smelled like Drew, and rather than scowl and get pissed, my insides went all warm and wet again, tempting me just to get myself off already so I could rest. I needed to get laid. Badly.

I ran my hand down over my pubic bone, finding my crotch hot and damp through the leggings. "He killed Mom," I reminded myself under my breath. Self-hatred rose, and I jerked my hand away.

I would not masturbate to thoughts of that bastard.

Ever.

Eyes clenched shut, I rolled to my stomach and let out a huff. To keep my pissiness alive, I relived memories of Mom, reminded myself of the picture album I'd created while in my teens so I would never forget her, and the family photo of us on my bed stand back at my apartment.

I remembered the good times with both my parents—going out for dinner at fancy restaurants, the time we went to Canobie Lake. Our first vacation to Europe where I got to see all the sights, the time Dad had bought the Italian villa—but Drew had been with us every minute, his presence ensuring our safety.

It was a long time before my mind quieted.

———

I run like the wind, free and focused on moving. Giggles spill from my lips as my legs pump, taking me toward the pines alongside the playground Daddy would meet us at.

"Shaun!" Mommy calls after me, but I don't stop.

My sneakers smack the pebbled walkway, and I giggle again. The new bodyguard lingered in the parking lot to smoke, and the second Mommy got me out of the car, I shot off across the playground like a rocket, trying for a few seconds of freedom from non-stop rules and watchful eyes.

Freedom beckons from the trees—and I won't be stopped.

The shade's coolness slips over me as I enter the woods, but an arm shoots out from behind one massive trunk, yanking me off my feet and cutting off my laughter.

Kicking earns me a clobber to the head. Biting a hairy arm earns me a smack across the face.

"Mommy!" I shriek, still fighting like my big teddy bear taught me to do.

"Shaun!"

I settle a bit at her voice being so near, but seconds later, land face down in the dirt. Gunshots sound and I curl into a ball, hands over my ears, eyes clenching shut against the loud booms over my head.

They can't see me if I can't see them...

"No!" Daddy hollers, and I know everything is going to be okay—

———

I jerked upright, my heart pounding in my chest, and slapped a hand over my mouth to keep from sobbing.

Mommy...

A sob tore loose anyway as the grief I'd experienced as a young girl slammed back into me. Daddy had been there to hold me close, shelter me from seeing what I shouldn't. But no such arms had offered support after that day.

I curled back up on Drew's bed, choking on sobs.

"Shaun?"

I wanted to scream at him to go away, curse him for not being with us that day—but couldn't catch my breath.

"Shit."

The bed dipped beside me, and I found myself yanked up into strong arms. Warmth. He murmured words of probable bullshit I couldn't make out over the sobs ripping from me. Although I wished for a knife to stab into Drew's back for not being with us that day, I found myself holding onto his shirt, soaking his chest with my tears.

Clinging to him, to his offer of consolation that I'd been yearning for and never received from my dad.

Turning my focus on hating him proved hard with the memory of what had happened that day fresh in my mind, but it's what eventually stopped my tears. I focused on breathing, easing the trembling in my body—but Drew held me close, and my hormones, damn them, took note of his hard chest, his band-like arms, and gentle fingers running through my hair.

He smelled so fucking good I wanted to lick him from beard to balls. His body felt so damn perfect surrounding me that I wanted to bury my soul inside him to escape the reality of my life. Along with the lingering grief and guilt in the pit of my stomach.

But I also wanted to stop the heart beating beneath my cheek. I wanted to hurt him for what he'd done.

"I'm so sorry," he whispered against my hair as though admitting his own guilt.

My own eased a bit at his words—but I wouldn't forgive him. Ever. No matter what he said, no matter what he did.

A shuddered breath settled over me, and I rested against him for just a moment longer, soaking in his warmth even as it roused my body to life.

"I should have been there," he continued, and I knew I must have cried out in my sleep, revealing what I'd dreamed. "You and Joanna were mine to protect. Mine." His voice caught, but I wouldn't allow a stitch of empathy to rise at his display of grief. "I should have been there…"

He'd loved Mom—Dad had told me as much—but the pain in his voice made me realize just how *much*.

An idea, one I should have obliterated to atoms the second it whispered in my mind, fluttered to life and quickly took formation.

His hot breath against my forehead as I slowly pulled my head back spiked my arousal regardless of my thoughts toward him, and I hated it. Desiring him felt so wrong—how could I want him inside me when I wanted him dead? Conflicting feelings ransacked my body, but one overshadowed them all —lust.

I peered up into his dark eyes, determined to kill the heart beating against my palm I placed where my cheek had been. I would have my cake in the end —but in the meantime, I had every intention of eating his.

Drew brushed my hair from my face, blinking his eyes to focus on my mouth. "Shaun—"

I leaned in and kissed him, cutting off my whispered name from his lips. Only a second's hesitation and he tangled his fingers in my hair, taking control. A tug stung my scalp, and my lips parted on a gasp even as his roughness sent a rush of wetness to coat my panties.

He dominated my mouth, my tongue, groaning, and stealing my breath. With a mere kiss, he obliterated to fragments every thought I'd had, corrupted the plan to steal his heart and stomp on it, the underlying grief that induced said plan.

I breathed in his sweet breath. Whimpered against his lips while wiggling in his hold to straddle his thighs.

Thick, powerful thighs... Another whimper slipped from me as I pressed against his hard cock.

Oh holy hell.

My pussy spasmed at the thought of having his long length buried inside me.

One hand in my hair, the other dropping to my ass, he grasped me tight, his arms a cage of muscle and steel. Lust and madness.

My body burned for him.

And, he pulled away so abruptly, setting me aside, that I squeaked while falling onto my back. Drew stood beside the bed, looming over me, hands clenched at his sides. His hair stuck up wild as though I'd run my hands through it—I probably had, but couldn't remember anything beyond his taste, the soft touch of his beard, and the need throbbing between my legs.

"I'm sorry—"

"I'm not," I whispered, cutting him off, my pulse thundering, my lungs feeling starved of air.

"I don't want this, Shaun."

A smirk flirted with a corner of my lips, and I relaxed back onto the bed, my thighs parting while I lifted an eyebrow.

His beard twitched as though he clenched his jaw.

I expected him to spew all the reasons we couldn't fuck, how my dad would kill him, blah,

blah, blah ... but he spun on his heel and disappeared into the hallway.

Point, me, I thought, my smile growing even though disappointment over not getting what I wanted—*right then, damnit*—pissed me off.

He couldn't deny wanting me—his hard cock and hungry mouth refuted his words. I might not be the most experienced woman on the block, but I knew the weapons in my arsenal. Knew how to move my body, knew how to get a man's attention, and fill his eyes with lust.

Drew Tellier wouldn't escape me. I'd been gifted the perfect opportunity, the exact looks of the woman he lamented losing, and nothing would stop me from taking advantage of that fact.

And making him pay.

6

—————

DREW

Goddamnit all to fucking hell and back.

I stormed down the stairs, intent on the bottle of whiskey above the fridge. Kissing Shaun had tightened my entire body to the point of pain, zinging enough energy through me to power a hundred fucking light bulbs.

My hands shook as I poured a good dose of whiskey into a glass, and I slammed the drink down, still cursing myself. Cursing my weakness. Cursing Ben for dumping his daughter in my lap.

"Fuck," I swore again at the memory of her grinding against my dick and closed my eyes as I set the glass down on the counter. She'd tasted so damn sweet, so damn innocent although she hadn't moved like one. Her ass in my hand, her silky strands wrapped around my fingers...

I let out a slow, hissed exhale, fighting to get myself under control. My dick ached. Balls brewed, ready to explode.

If I didn't get a change of scenery, get some goddamn space from Shaun, I would end up fucking her. No question about it.

I couldn't do that to Joanna's memory, or break Ben's trust in such a way.

"Get dressed, Shaun!" I hollered, staring at the ceiling my mind made up. "We're heading to the club!"

She didn't reply, but I heard her feet hit the floor and the bathroom door closing seconds later

She came downstairs after a short time, her hair in a ponytail and flip flops on her feet.

"You need some goddamn shoes," I grunted, pulling on a sweatshirt.

"Your whore friend didn't bring me any."

Lips pursed, I grabbed the keys. "Her name is Tina."

"Don't give a shit."

"Let's go," I muttered rather than give her shit about her attitude.

We made our way out of the woods, and I steeled

myself for what I needed to say. "I'm not going to fuck you."

She didn't respond but peered at the fogging passenger window.

"I loved your mother, and I won't break your father's trust."

Still, she kept silent like a petulant child, arms crossed and all. Little brat needed to learn some manners. My hands itched to take on that task, but I clenched the steering wheel tighter, deciding our one-way conversation could go to hell. I'd said what I needed to.

We drove in silence the rest of the way as disgust over what I'd done, what I had allowed, continued to simmer inside me, brewing into an ugly mess.

For a late afternoon on a Saturday, the club seemed kinda quiet. Guess too many boys sat home hungover from the party that raged the night before. At least a couple of the old ladies had cleaned the place up. Still smelled like cigarettes and booze like always, though.

I caught sight of Tina across the club and nodded my thanks again.

She hopped up and sauntered forward as I dragged Shaun into the club. "Hey, Warden." She touched my cut lightly with her blood-red fingernails. "I'm ready to collect—if you're up for it."

The twinkle in Tina's eye didn't entice me near as much as the growl at my back.

"Not now," I told her, pushing past and ignoring her annoyed huff.

Greed, one of my employees sat at the bar with a glass of cranberry juice, the pussy. "'Sup?" he asked as I ushered Shaun toward him.

"Shaun needs a babysitter while I talk to Vigil," I told him.

Shaun let out the huff I'd expected but plunked her fine ass down on the seat beside Greed. "Hey," she said, offering him a dazzling smile.

My gaze narrowed at the fact she'd offer him one but not me.

"I'm Shaun," she said, holding out her hand.

"Hey, back. I'm Cody, but my brothers call me Greed." Greed did a quick once-over, burning my fucking blood. He loved pussy more than most—and never had any issues getting some with his pretty boy eyelashes and flashing grin.

"Keep your fucking hands to yourself, Greed."

"Gotcha, boss man."

"And you stay put," I told Shaun through clenched teeth and spun on my heel.

"So who are you and what are you doing here, fine thing?" I heard Greed asked as I stalked away.

I moved beyond hearing, thank fuck, since the thought of her flirting with him in return knifed my gut—even if she did it out of jealousy.

Dream on.

I yanked open Vigil's door without knocking.

"The fuck is up your ass?" he growled as I slammed the door shut behind me.

Ryker sat on the couch, sprawled out, his scowl as deep as mine.

"Sorry about last night," I told him, needing that shit behind me so I could focus on the future.

A muscle ticked in his jaw, but he nodded. "We're good."

I turned back to Vigil. "Ryker tell you what happened after you left last night?"

"Yep."

Expelling a heavy breath, I sat in the chair across from Vigil. He peered at me with pale eyes, cold and seemingly empty. The man was a beast, same as Ryker, just as deadly, and just as mean, a real vigilante in badass form. Other than my own two fists, they'd be the first brothers I'd want at my back—besides Stone with his indifferent feelings and black belt in karate.

"Thode's daughter, huh?" Vigil asked.

I nodded. "Been friends with the fucker for a long ass time."

"Ryker says he's fucked."

My chest tightened, fearing that truth, yet wishing it otherwise. "He wouldn't accept help."

"Good." Vigil sat back, his stare still on my face as my gut hardened. "Last thing we need is to get on the wrong side of a goddamn cartel family."

The Vipers didn't run illegal drugs, but we had our hands in some shady shit, same as every other biker outlaw gang. The chop shop, extortion, the money laundering... We didn't need to feed the goddamn drug epidemic killing people left and right.

"It's tough letting a brother head into danger on his own," I muttered.

"Tell me about him."

I started at the beginning—with Joanna. I ended with the spitting image of her currently sitting at the bar out in the lounge.

"You gonna claim her when her daddy doesn't come back?"

I fought the desire to curse Vigil out. Giving up hope, regardless of the mess Ben probably would find himself in, wasn't an option.

"I'll take her off your hands if you can't handle her," Ryker said, jerking my head around.

"The fuck you will."

He grinned, his light eyes full of shit rather than death for a change. "Sick fuck," he said, chuckling.

I wanted to punch the fucker, but couldn't argue with him, either.

"Drew sticking his dick into her young pussy isn't sick in my book," Vigil said. "She ain't her mom."

"Far from it." I crossed my arms, my head full of memories. "Joanna was a sweet soul, the kind you want to keep barefoot and pregnant in the kitchen. She'd have loved that life, too. Had it with Ben until I fucked up."

Neither brother said a word to refute the truth and ease my guilty conscious.

"Shaun's a sassy bitch with a foul mouth and zero manners," I continued, focusing on her rather than my mistakes, my life's number one regret.

"A rich little girl who has had her life rocked to shit," Ryker said. "Her dad didn't seem to notice or care about her last night if you ask me. Maybe that's the reason she's acting out."

"It's more than that," I said, remembering her wildness as a kid. "She wasn't good at listening. Always looking for a way out. Freedom."

"Little wildcat, huh?" Vigil asked, one brow raised.

His kind of woman—same as Ryker. "You don't fucking touch her either," I said, unable to keep the threat from my tone.

"Touchy, touchy, touchy," he said with a rare smirk.

"Fuck." I scrubbed a hand down over my face. "What the hell am I going to do?"

"Fuck her," Ryker said.

I ignored our Sergeant at Arms while Vigil studied me, his lips flat-lining. "You're going to do what you promised Ben because you're a man of your fucking word," Vigil said. "Got any way to track him? Any way to reach him to know what the fuck is going on?"

"Not a goddamn thing."

"Devil out there when you came in?" Vigil asked, tilting his head toward the office door.

I shook my head.

Vigil grabbed his cell, his brow furrowed while dialing. "Devil—you on the compound?"

An affirmative mumble reached my ears.

"Get your ass in the office."

Vigil tossed his cell aside, and minutes later, Devil sauntered in, a black, leather bag over his shoulder. He looked more like a goddamn CEO than biker, with his smooth chin and perfectly arranged hair. The damn hawk nose in the middle of his face kept him from being pretty like Greed, though.

He'd earned his biker name for being a sneaky fucker, one who could wile a computer into giving him what he wanted. Many an unsuspecting souls sold theirs to Devil in the form of wired funds. Hush money.

"What's up?" he asked, sprawling onto the seat beside me.

"Fire that laptop up," Vigil said. "You're going to impress the hell outta me with your hacking skills."

"Don't I always?" Devil shot back with a grin while opening his bag.

Twenty long as fuck minutes later, the cocky fucker even raised my eyebrows.

"How the fuck did you do that?" I asked, staring at the computer screen showing live video feed our government would kill for.

"I'll never tell," Devil said, scrolling and clicking on images of an opulent home. The fucker had hacked into Arturo's home security system.

Arturo had dozens of cameras around and inside his estate—but no images showed Ben or evidence of torture—or Arturo, for that matter. While a few of

Arturo's men stood around guarding the place, the house appeared vacant.

"Nothing," I muttered, sitting back in my chair.

"Arturo's cousin grew up in Southie," Ryker said from behind me as he peered over my shoulder at Devil's laptop propped on Vigil's desk. "I know some people ... could make some calls."

I glanced at Vigil, once more holding my fucking breath to see how far he would go to help me out. The Vipers stayed out of the cartel's shit—but would he bend for a brother?

Vigil's stare burrowed into my goddamn head, making me twitchy as fuck, but I kept my ass from shifting. "Quietly," he finally answered Ryker.

"Don't I always?"

Vigil snorted. "You don't do *anything* quietly."

"I don't *fuck* quietly," he corrected our president with a chuckle. "I could slide a knife between Arturo's ribs without a goddamn sound, though, given the chance."

"Wish you would," I muttered, knowing he could take life without pause, without question, without a goddamn noise past his lips. I'd seen it enough times in my years with the Vipers. "Then all this shit would be over," I said. "Shaun could go about her merry fucking way, and I—"

"Could go back to being a miserable fucker," Devil cut me off.

"Fuck you."

"No, thanks." He grinned, and I stood as Ryker and Vigil moved back to their seats.

"Gonna hang around for a bit with that leggy wildcat?" Ryker called out as I opened the door, spilling in the sound of heavy metal and balls breaking on the pool tables in the lounge beyond.

"Yep." I slammed the door behind me, quickly scanning the room.

Shaun leaned over a pool table, lining a shot—and Greed was all up her ass, bent over her back, showing her where to hit the cue.

Fucking red flashed through my sight.

I grabbed hold of his cut and yanked him back quick as fuck.

"The fuck—" He saw my face and clamped his lips shut, straightening his vest.

Shaun sent me a sassy smirk while standing, the ball she'd shot clinking into a pocket. "Problem?" she asked sweetly as I shoved Greed aside.

"You fucking touch her again, I'll rip your goddamn arms off," I whispered, and Greed backed off, hands held up.

"Got it, boss man."

A few brothers at the table beside us chuckled, and I shot a glare their way. They returned to their game, smiles fading quick as fuck.

"Let's go," I told Shaun, grabbing her arm.

She stumbled after me in her goddamn flip flops, but didn't put up a fight, thank fuck.

I was fucking gone on the girl—and everyone in the damn club had seen it.

Ryker needed to make those goddamn calls and find Ben, so I could help him do what he needed to do in order to get his daughter out of my life—so I could be a miserable, lonely fuck again.

7

SHAUN

Fucking asshole, I muttered in my head—again—while staring out the passenger window. Drew had made one hell of a show at the club, his jealousy so damn obvious and sexy as fuck, my body climbed aboard the "hell yeah" train.

I'd been having a good time for the first time in almost twenty-four hours, enjoying Greed—Cody's—attention, his flirting, and sly hands, but the second Drew yanked him off me, I knew I was in trouble.

I wanted Drew, and not just to get into his head and heart in order to crush both. The man was ripe for the plucking, even his brothers had seen that, and while I knew I could impale myself on his massive cock eventually, the thought of how it might affect me emotionally scared the shit out of me.

I'd be better off running for my life, chasing freedom like I always did.

"I haven't heard anything about your dad," Drew finally said, breaking the heavy silence in his truck's warming cab.

I didn't bother replying since my throat tightened—with fear and *more* guilt. *Here I sit thinking about sitting on Drew's cock while my dad could very well be getting pieces of his body hacked off.*

"We have eyes on the cartel's compound—there's nothing to indicate Ben's even been there yet."

I managed a nod, not knowing if Drew saw, but still couldn't find my voice to reply.

"One of my brothers knows some people, though," Drew continued, his voice holding a hint of empathy I wouldn't expect from an outlaw biker even if we did have history. "Hopefully, we'll hear something soon."

The dark landscape breezed past the window as my knotted stomach threatened to bring back up the slice of cold, leftover pizza I'd had at the club thanks to Greed's hospitality.

We rode in silence the rest of the way, and

exhaustion pulled on my eyelids again, even though it couldn't have been more than seven at night.

I followed Drew into his kitchen, coming to a standstill as he tossed his keys onto the counter and pulled a bottle of whiskey from the cabinet above the fridge.

"Want a drink?" he asked, grabbing two glasses from another cabinet.

"I'm not twenty-one yet."

He snorted and poured. "Like that fact stopped you before. You stank of booze last night when your dad dropped you off."

I glared at him but took the offered drink. "Krystal and I were out dancing at *Benny's*, I'll have you know—I wasn't drinking."

"Whatever, sweetheart." Drew studied me while sipping, and I held his gaze while doing the same. My throat fucking burned, but I swallowed against the coughs wanting to hack my lungs.

He smirked, his eyes lighting, reminding me so much of the man I knew when I'd been younger, that a part of me softened toward him. "Good shit, isn't it?"

I shrugged and sipped again while he tipped his head back, finishing the drink in one swallow.

Knowing I'd never be able to do the same, I moseyed into the living room, glass in hand.

"Where were you that day?" I asked, sitting my ass down and pinning him with a stare while kicking off the whore's flip flops. She'd fucking touched him at the club earlier—and that fact pissed me the hell off for some stupidly insane reason.

Drew's brow furrowed, and he poured another drink before sitting down on the couch beside me. He held his glass in one hand, bottle in the other. "I was in a woman's bed."

"So, you were fucking some woman when you were supposed to be protecting my mom and me."

He tossed back his double. "Yep."

"Selfish fuck."

"Call me every name in the book you want, Shaun—I've cursed myself a million times worse."

Another poured shot went down his throat.

Rather than rant and rave, attack, and rip out his eyes like I wanted to, I sat quietly, sipping while he slammed the shots back.

"She was a lovely lady, your mom," Drew said after yet another drink, his focus on the amber liquid once more in the bottom of his tumbler, his voice laced with remorse and guilt, same as every time he mentioned the past. "One of a kind." That whiskey, too, also made it down his throat, and I sipped again.

"I've never been more fucking sorry for something in my miserable life," he muttered, pouring another.

I sat back while he reminisced, his words starting to slur, trying like hell to keep my heart from thawing at the confessions pouring from his mouth. He'd loved her first—he'd had her first, something I hadn't known. They'd taken one another's virginities, but their relationship ended the next day because he'd stepped out of the picture when my dad told him how much he'd fallen in love with my mom.

"You gave her up without a fight?" I asked, realizing I'd drank too much if I was willingly conversing with the asshole.

"Yep." Another shot down the hatch. "Didn't touch another woman until that day I skipped out on my responsibilities."

My mind spun to calculate. "You went without sex for ten years? After only ... one time?"

"Celibate as fuck."

I eyed the almost empty bottle then eyed Drew studying the drained glass in his hand, more than a little surprised he'd gone so long without fucking another woman after my mom.

"Thank you," I finally said.

Drew jerked his head up at my whispered words. "What?"

"Thank you for letting Dad have her."

He blinked a few times as though processing I thanked him for allowing me life.

"I should have been there." His beard twitched as though he clenched his jaw.

Seizing the opportunity, I leaned toward him and palmed his cheek, his beard soft against my hand.

He closed his eyes and leaned into my touch as my fingers buried into his whiskers.

I wouldn't offer what he probably longed to hear me say, but pretending to do so would be easy as hell since my damn heart softened even more. I scooted closer and kissed him.

With a growl, he took up where we'd left off earlier in the day, yanking me onto his lap, the bottle and glass falling, one or both shattering on the floor. I couldn't be bothered to find out as he attacked my mouth, claiming my tongue, stealing my breath and thoughts again.

My body buzzed along with my head as I ground against his growing erection, wetness and hell yeahs growing between my thighs. I reached between us and grabbed his hard length.

"Fuck," he whispered harshly against my lips, thrusting into my hold.

"Please," I whispered back with the intent to make him fall—not because my pussy pulsed at the thought of having his girth stretch me. Nope.

"Goddamnit, Shaun."

Once more, I found myself set aside in a flash, my lips tingling, my panties soaked, nipples straining for his teeth.

"Not gonna fuck you." His voice lacked conviction as he ran his hands through his hair.

I yanked my sweatshirt off overhead and leaned back, crooking a finger at him.

"No."

"You want to," I told him, sliding my hand beneath the band of my leggings and finding myself soaked as expected. "My pussy is wet for you," I whispered and gasped while sliding a finger deep inside me.

He groaned and clamped his eyes shut, tipping his head back. "Get upstairs in bed. Now."

"Coming with me?" I asked, pun totally intended.

"No." He met my gaze rather than watch me finger myself. "Go to bed, Shaun."

"I'd rather you shove your big dick deep inside me."

"You don't know what you're asking for," he said, his tone low and sexy as fuck, his looming body trembling as though on the verge of losing his shit and taking what he and his bulging cock obviously wanted.

"Oh, I think I do." I smiled up at him but bit my lip while lifting my hips to meet my plunging finger.

Darkness filled his eyes, the type that would scare the shit out of me had it been another man. I wondered if a wild beast raged inside him and what sorts of naughtiness he imagined doing with me.

My three vanilla experiences had left me wanting, and the idea of more, of experience beyond a young college guy, raced my pulse.

I pulled my hand from beneath my leggings and held it out to Drew.

What man would say no?

Drew the asshole, apparently. The heat diminished from his eyes as though sudden soberness slammed into his brain. He turned away, stepping over the shattered glass and spilled whiskey.

As though I didn't sit there wet, willing, and

waiting for his cock, he grabbed a roll of paper towels and a broom.

I watched as he started to clean up the glass and liquor mess.

Seriously?

With a huff, I stood and stalked around him, stomped up the stairs, and did as my babysitter had ordered, the fucking asshole.

I went to bed. Alone.

———

I woke a few hours later, horny as hell. Hot and bothered. My head still slightly buzzed, but I knew exactly what I was doing while slipping out of Drew's bed, stripping naked, and sneaking down the stairs.

A small nightlight from the kitchen kept me from stumbling through the dark, but I pulled up short when I rounded the couch.

Drew lay sprawled on his back, shirtless, the throw blanket low enough on his hips I knew he didn't wear a stitch of clothing beneath. Wishing for more light to study the ink on his torso, I moved in closer, my fingertips tingling to touch, my mouth watering to taste.

He'd said no a few hours earlier, but he'd been lying to both of us.

I grasped the edge of the blanket and slipped it off his body. My stare fixated on his cock as the blanket fell soundlessly to the floor. Even flaccid, he appeared bigger than the younger guys I'd had. I imagined his length swelled fully, and my pussy spasmed.

A quick glance up showed his face still slack with sleep.

I sank to my knees beside the couch, my pulse thrumming, and returned my focus on what I wanted—what I needed. Not bothering to take the chance he'd wake quickly from a brush of fingers across his cock, I went all in, closed my mouth over the head, and lathed at his musky taste.

He shifted.

I grasped his base to keep him from jerking away and sucked.

He groaned, stiffening against my tongue.

Smiling around his girth, I took him deeper.

Fingers tangled in my messy ponytail, but Drew didn't yank me off his cock. He cursed, harsh and wicked while holding my head close to his groin, swelling fully to gag me.

Damnit. Tears instantly sprang to my eyes, but I

held still, allowed him to choke me with his thick head. *Whatever it takes...*

He tightened his hold in my hair, stinging my scalp, and slowly pulled my face away from his body. I licked, nipped, and sucked, and the second the rim of his cock reached the insides of my lips, he shoved me back down his length, fucking deep into my throat and gagging me once more.

I told myself wetness didn't well between my thighs because of his aggression, his dominance—it was simply need from having gone so long without.

Lies.

Twice more, he pulled me off his dick only to slam my face back into his groin.

"Fuck, Shaun—you don't know what you're asking for."

Oh, but I could imagine. "Give it to me," I garbled around his girth as he allowed me to breathe once more.

Give in, let me steal your heart and crush it beneath my heel.

8

DREW

She didn't just wake me from sleep, Shaun woke the raging beast inside me, the one desperate for a taste of her young body, the one who wanted to feast—take—leaving nothing untouched.

Anger gritted my teeth, but she'd taken me past the point of saying no, the sassy brat. She wanted my cock. She would get it.

I shoved into her throat over and over, the sounds of her gagging and moaning around my girth, tightening my balls. She was no pro, but the effort she put into sucking my dick earned her points. She'd learn—and I would be the one to teach her.

Later.

I needed her pussy wrapped around me.

I yanked her off me with a pop, squeezing the base of my dick to calm the fuck down. We stared at one another in the dim nightlight, tear tracks lining her cheeks from gagging so damn much. She'd stripped down to bare skin, and what a fucking sight she was. Pert tits, strawberry-like nipples hard with need. On her goddamn knees beside me.

I sat up. "Spoiled little brat," I said, yanking on her hair and tugging her close to my face so I could make out her eyes in the darkness. "Your daddy probably didn't punish you enough."

Her smirk only pissed me off more.

"I'll give you what you think you want," I promised with zero trace of anything but warning in my voice, "but you'll be sorry."

A flit of wariness crossed her face, but I was past the point of caring. Without another word, I stood and tossed her over my shoulder, the scent of her arousal so damn close to my face, my mouth watered.

"I'm going to take it all, Shaun. Every goddamn inch of you and make you wish you'd left well enough alone."

She tensed, and I smacked her ass—hard.

Shaun hissed, punching my back, but I ignored her ineffectual hits and strode up the stairs, my leaking dick leading the way.

"Put me down!"

Teeth gritted against the pissiness and lust warring inside me, I smacked her ass twice more.

"You—you can't manhandle me like this, you bastard!"

"You asked for it." I turned on my bedroom light and tossed her onto my bed. "And I'm not going to stop until you *beg* for it."

She scrambled backward—but I wasn't having it. I grabbed her ankle, yanking her out flat once more, and laid down on top of her, trapping her beneath me. Her eyes flashed while she sneered up at me.

"This what you want?" I asked, grinding my dick against her pelvis.

"Get off me!" She dug her fingernails into my back, refuting her words, her thighs widening to accommodate me.

"I don't do impulsive," I said, smearing my pre-cum all over her belly while grabbing her arms and holding them over her head, "but you..."

I nosed her neck, breathing in the scent of my soap and her softness beneath, groaning. "Goddamn, I smell good on you."

"Fucker."

Chuckling, I nipped along her jaw. "I plan on it."

I sat and flipped her in one move, straddling her thighs to keep her in place.

"What are you—"

I swatted her firm ass, cutting her off.

"Damnit!" she shrieked, and I smacked again in the same damn spot. "Drew!" She twisted and writhed, trying to get her hands on me, but I once more grasped them over her head, leaning down to bite her earlobe.

"You deserve a hell of a lot more than a red ass, so shut the fuck up and take your punishment like a goddamn grownup."

I yanked her arms behind her back and held her wrists in one hand, high enough she strained, whimpering.

Sliding down her thighs allowed me better access to skin—and I let her have it. She shrieked and squirmed, but nothing she did or said stopped me from making good on my promise.

My handprints looked fine as fuck on her smooth skin. Branded. But not yet claimed. She didn't relent or fall pliant until my hand stung. Moans began to escape her parted lips, the tears soaking my pillow ceasing.

"Please," I barely made out her whisper, but my balls ached, making me decide that one word was begging enough for what I'd promised.

I released my firm hold on her wrists, flipped her over once more, and she went willingly, blinking up at me through wet eyelashes, although her backside had to sting like fuck.

"Not so sassy now," I said, stroking down my aching length while settling on my knees between her lax thighs.

Her gaze dropped to my hand.

"That's right, Shaun." I smeared pre-cum down my length. "My dick is fucking hard—for you."

"My dad is going to kill you," she whispered, the lust in her eyes tightening my balls up against my body.

"He won't for the spanking—but he will for this." I leaned over her and shoved into her sopping pussy with one thrust.

She shrieked, her thighs and nails clamping onto me at the same time.

Holy fucking mother of God.

So damn tight—

I pulled out and slammed in again, a grunt ripping from my chest at the sheer perfection of her tight pussy.

Those long ass legs wrapped around my waist, and I let loose, giving over to the beast inside me. I knew once I took what I wanted, I would never let her go—too fucking late to stop. Her slick wetness eased my thrusts, her whimpers and heels pulling me in every time I pulled out fueled the fire brewing inside me.

"More," she gasped as I slammed against her cervix.

I took her mouth in a bruising kiss, and she gave as good as she got, her teeth nipping, her fingers grasping onto my hair and beard to keep me close.

"Come all over my dick, Shaun," I said against her mouth, grinding my pelvis against hers. "Soak my cock."

"M-more..." She writhed beneath me, and I reached between us, giving her what her firm little nub needed while thrusting hard and fast.

One pinch to her clit and she bowed beneath me. "Oh, fuck!" Her pussy clamped down on my dick, and a rush of wetness leaked around me. I slammed into her over and over. Teeth clenched to keep from blowing my load.

Pulling out of her tight heat hurt like hell, but I wanted her on her knees. She went willingly, and I slammed into her from behind, pressing her entire front side into my mattress, her sweet pussy even tighter with her thighs pressed together.

"You're fucking mine, Shaun." My balls spasmed at my declaration, and I pulled out to shoot all over her back, grunting as I milked every spurt from my shaft. "Mine." One last shudder and I leaned over her with one hand beside her shoulder, my head hanging as I caught my breath.

She lay unmoving beneath me except for the pants of her own breath fluttering the strands of dark hair that had fallen over her parted lips.

With a groan, I sat back on my haunches, taking in the ropes of white stripes across her back.

Mine.

I smeared my spunk all over her back and ass, her hiss as I kneaded the redness on her cheeks and thighs, satisfying the demon inside me.

"You're a bastard," she muttered.

Even though there was no heat or anger in her voice, her words hit me like a slap to my face.

I'd fucked Joanna's daughter. Brutally so without a thought to her experience and smeared my goddamn cum all over her ass like I had a point to prove.

I jerked my sticky hands off her body, my teeth once more clenched.

You sick fuck.

Guilt slammed into me like an uppercut to my sternum. She'd begged, and I'd taken—but I was no asshole when it came to aftercare.

9

SHAUN

"Stay here," Drew muttered while sliding off the bed

One command I would gladly obey. Unable to move, I managed to flutter my hair from across my mouth with a few huffed breaths.

Drew left me for the bathroom, and I listened to water run, my mind and body still buzzing from the fuck of my life. I smiled against his pillow, so damn satisfied—with myself, not just Drew and his cock. He'd claimed me like a damn caveman, his growls of "mine" shivering over my skin, but I hadn't bothered refuting. That would come later.

Point, set.

The big bad biker boy had handed over his heart, and it was mine to do with as I wished.

I'd expected him to be rough, had feared it a bit, to be honest, but his hands on me, his forceful taking...

My pussy spasmed at the memory of his sudden intrusion with no regard for possible virginity or birth control, and I bit my lower lip, turned on again when I should have been pissed. Horrified, even.

Drew was no college boy, that was for damn sure, and the memory of how he moved between my thighs took over whatever care I had about having unprotected sex.

He returned, wiping his sticky branding off my back and ass where he'd rubbed it in, and I found myself melting further into his bed at his unexpected, gentle touch, exhaustion pulling on me.

"Did I hurt you?" he asked, his voice low and soft with concern while rubbing some sort of cream over my sore backside.

"Yes." *But it was fucking awesome.*

No words of apology for his brutal taking followed our short exchange, and I realized I didn't want one.

He finished and laid down beside me, pulling the comforter I'd left askew earlier atop both of us.

I might have won the battle, but a war still loomed, of that, I had no doubt. When he wrapped his arms around me, I went willingly to snuggle against him, his warmth, his hard chest and arms, his luscious scent filling my lungs. It'd been so damn long since a man had held me in such a way—comforting just for the sake of holding me. Protective. I soaked it in like a parched sponge.

Drew kissed the top of my head. "Sleep. We'll talk in the morning."

We'll do a hell of a lot more than talk if I have my way.

I closed my eyes and obeyed, floating away on the high he'd given me.

———

Daddy sobs, his hands over his eyes.

I peer up at him, shivering from the cold, my throat aching. Tugging on his black suit coat doesn't get his attention, and I blink tears from my eyes while turning back for one last goodbye to Mommy.

A black box is all I can see—and that slowly disappears into a cold hole in the ground.

No more hugs. No more kisses.

Another tear slips down my cheek, and I look up at daddy, needing his attention, needing him to tell me that everything is going to be okay.

He turns and stalks away, and after one last glance at the dark hole, I scurry after him, the wet leaves blanketing the cemetery, soaking my Mary Janes. I slip my hand into his, but he pulls away and makes a call while striding past gravestones that sit as silent as the bodies buried beneath.

My breath fogs as I fight to keep from sobbing like he'd done. Daddy doesn't know I ran away from mommy at the park. He doesn't know it's my fault she rested in a box without light, without color. Without a heartbeat or fogging breath like I still have.

"She's gone," he says a second later into his cell, and I bite my lip, hating that he's been angry ever since mommy died. "I hope whoever the whore was that kept you from doing your job was worth it," Daddy spit the words, and I ease back, putting a few feet between us in case he decides to turn his anger on me.

"It's your fault, Drew. Your fucking fault Joanna is gone." Daddy's voice breaks, and he shoves his cell into his coat.

Drew. Daddy's friend. My and Mommy's friend. My real-life teddy bear.

"Daddy?" I ask, reaching for his clenched fist.

Once more, he ignores me, and I stumble after him, wrapping my own arms around myself since he won't.

I woke with a start, my eyes stinging as I blinked in the sunlight pouring through open blinds.

Drew's bed.

His fault.

A hard swallow eased the rising grief a bit. Daddy hadn't hugged me in over ten years, and I'd taken comfort in the enemy's the night before without a damn thought about what he'd done. What he'd cost me.

Yes, I'd run from Mom that day—but if Drew had been with us, I never would have taken off. He'd been the uncle I never had, the big brother whose shoulders and strong arms had carried me wherever I'd wished as a kid.

He'd been my constant companion, my friend, when Dad hadn't been around to play with me.

I'd loved him once upon a time, and even though warm fuzzies began to snuggle inside me over childhood memories, I squashed them down.

Drew had cost me my mom. I'd do well to remember that truth.

Thank fuck he didn't sprawl on the bed beside me, because in that moment, I wanted to stab a ten-inch knife into his heart over and over.

Scowling over the lingering ache in my backside and between my thighs, I stalked across the bedroom, uncaring of wherever he'd taken off to.

The scent of coffee slammed into me as I stepped into the hallway, but I made for the bathroom rather than follow my nose to the best and only good thing about mornings.

One long, hot shower later, I contemplated clothing. Hands on my hips, I considered the other set of leggings the whore had brought.

The war would continue—eventually—but I had some words for that asshole first.

I donned a pair of panties and a long tunic the whore must have thought I'd use to sleep in, and I made my way downstairs, needing coffee more than I needed air.

My skin pebbled a second before I saw Drew sitting on the couch, facing me, sipping his coffee. His dark eyes tracked my descent, but I turned away at the rush of heat dampening my clean panties.

Cursing him in my head, I poured coffee into a mug he'd left out for me. Even the sugar and jug of milk sat alongside.

Self-hatred over fucking a man I hated, and perhaps a little pissiness at Drew's newly-found hospitality—because of a good fuck, probably—

brewed inside me, darker than the coffee I drooled over.

Still scowling, I turned and leaned against the counter, ignoring the energy zapping between us while closing my eyes and sipping.

His cock had satisfied me ten times more than that first sip, I realized as the hot liquid settled in my stomach.

I glared across the cabin at that thought and sipped again, hoping to prove myself wrong.

Nope.

Drew stood, and I refused to gawk at the low-slung gray sweats hanging on his hips or the ripple of muscle leading up to hard pecs I'd snuggled against the night before. Veins, and dips and valleys…

Goddamn him.

"Someone woke up on the wrong side of the bed this morning," he said with a chuckle, and I stepped aside, thinking he reached for me.

He took the coffee carafe instead with another chuckle that deepened my scowl.

"You seem quite pleased with yourself this morning," I said, watching him in my periphery while lifting my mug for another swallow. "Taking advantage of me like that—"

He slammed the coffee pot back down and got in my face, pressing my back against the countertop.

"I woke to *you* sucking my *dick*, Shaun," he hissed. "*Without* my consent."

The fucker stole my tongue. I set aside my coffee while wracking my brain for a good comeback.

"You want to pretend you didn't ask for it to ease your conscious?" His pissy glare singed me.

"Don't pretend to read my mind," I said, a tremble in my voice rather than the fire I'd hoped for.

"You can't deny how wet your pussy was for me, Shaun. You can't deny squirting your cum all over my dick while I fucked you."

Heat flooded my face.

"I'll bet you're just as wet right now, aren't you?"

Drew grabbed my pussy through the shirt, and I gasped at the stinging ache from his harsh groping.

"Mmm." He leaned against me, and my breath caught as his nose ran along my neck. Sniffing. Licking. His palm rubbing between my thighs. "Deny you're wet," he said against my ear, pebbling my skin again. "Tell me you didn't want my cock again—tell me you don't want me inside your tight hole right this second."

I grasped his shoulders against the sudden weakness in my knees. "Damn you, Drew."

He yanked up my shirt and shoved his hand beneath my panties and two fingers straight into my sore pussy.

"Fucking soaked," he groaned, and I shuddered as he stroked deep inside me, my eyelids falling closed as every cell in my body honed in on his rough touch. "Tell me how much you don't want this," Drew murmured, his breath hot against my ear as he twisted his hand, his fingertips rubbing along that special spot inside me none of those young college boys had been able to locate.

"Tell me you don't want this very thing." He pressed his thumb against my clit and rubbed hard.

My climax stole my breath. Shattered my mind, and I convulsed in his arms, crying out curses on him, riding his hand like a damn rodeo queen.

The second I sagged, he stepped away and shoved his drenched fingers between his lips, his dark eyes boring into mine. He groaned, sucking them clean, and slid them free from his mouth.

"Can't deny it, little brat." He picked up his coffee and turned away as though unfazed by the sexual tension wreaking havoc on my brain, my trembling body. "I've got work to do."

I struggled to catch my breath, my pulse thrumming, and my hands like a vise on the counter's edge beside my waist. I called him every imaginable name in my head but kept my lips clamped shut.

I'd woken something inside him that threatened my sanity—and turned me the hell on. Every inch between my thighs stung. Ached. And, I expected poking at the wild beast inside him would only have me pressed up against a wall or bent over his couch, his cock so far up my sore pussy I wouldn't be able to breathe.

Temptation...

I bit on my lip until I tasted blood. *It's a war, Shaun, not a feast of flesh.*

Hanging onto that thought, I picked up my coffee in my shaking hand and sashayed my way through the living room, ignoring him once more sitting on the couch with his laptop in front of him. Chin lifted, I went upstairs as though unfazed, same as him.

Winning rounds would be me spreading my thighs time and again. I just needed to keep a better focus on the end of our little war so he wouldn't fuck with my head like he had in that moment.

10

DREW

I fucked up.

Again.

But her sassy ass attitude demanded to be put in its place. My balls ached to release inside her pussy, her parentage be damned. I wanted to coat every inch of her with my cum. Mark and claim. Make her come around my dick until she lay lax and sweet, same as the night before.

She'd felt so damn good falling asleep in my arms like she'd been born to be there.

Cursing, I closed my eyes and pinched the bridge of my nose. I'd carried her around the first ten years of her life like she'd been my own daughter, and even though during those years, I'd never felt anything but protective over her, I couldn't help but feel like a sick bastard for my lusting over her.

Ben was going to kill me.

But my dick didn't care. Sure as fuck didn't care about the sixteen year difference, either.

A knock sounded on the front door, announcing the person my cameras had let me know drove up my driveway.

"'Bout fucking time," I muttered, setting my laptop aside.

Like a chicken shit, I'd called Stone, asking him to come over to talk about a potential client even though it was Sunday. I needed a goddamn buffer from the woman upstairs before I fucked her again.

I'd started up my personal security business while working for Ben, and once those ties between us had shattered, I'd taken my company along with me to the Vipers, hiring Stone, my best friend Sin, and later Greed to work for me. Our office was my home, using the club as a secondary place of business when needed, but I wasn't about to take Shaun back to where my brothers might hit on her—and end up with broken ribs or noses for even looking at her.

Ryker would flatten me for sure if I fucked up a brother.

Stone came in, scanning the place for threats out of habit, same as I always did regardless of knowing no one sat in wait. Learned instincts, same as he tried to teach at his dojo in self-defense classes.

"What's going on?" he asked while getting himself a cup of coffee.

I set my laptop on the kitchen table and made myself comfortable. I nodded toward the chair beside me, and he sat, his focus on my face.

"I'm in over my fucking head," I muttered with a scowl.

Stone sipped and waited.

"I fucked her last night." I kept my voice low.

"So?"

I shot a glare at him. "You know my history with Ben. Her mom."

"Again—so?"

A heavy exhale didn't ease the tension riding me. "She's off-limits."

"Obviously not."

"Goddamnit, Stone."

He shrugged, his glacial blue eyes seeing right through me. The fucker could read any soul he damn well pleased, intuitive prick. It's what made him the perfect sentinel for my army of four.

"You still want her?" he asked.

I nodded with a grimace.

"Then do it the right way—claim her."

"She's not what I want in an old lady. She's a feisty wildcat," I muttered the last bit, my shoulders stinging in memory of her fingernails.

He chuckled and rubbed the constant shadow of scruff lining his jaw. "Keep her away from Ryker—and Vigil for that matter."

A low growl rumbled my chest. "Either touches her, I'll slice their necks open."

Stone studied me, and I sat still, letting him see whatever the fuck he needed to. "You already claimed her."

"In my head, yes, but my heart tells me I'm a sick fuck and have no right to touch her."

He shrugged. "So I'm here to keep you from having to deal with your hard on. Got it."

Lips pursed, I turned my laptop toward him. "Burtonelli is running for office."

"Crooked fucker."

I nodded, but didn't give a shit since his politics would keep the law out of the Vipers' chop shop—and he'd forked over cash to Devil to keep the anonymous extortionist quiet about his shady dealings. "He's had two death threats and decided it was time to get someone to watch his ass."

"With Sin's bum arm, I'm assuming this one's mine?" Stone asked, scrolling through the file I'd put together.

"I'd take it, but Shaun is my priority right now."

Stone nodded and continued reading. "Putting Greed on this with me so the fucker can get more hours in?"

"Might as well." I got up to refill my coffee from the third pot I'd made, and my cell went off in the living room.

Ryker's name furrowed my brow. Knowing he must have news upped my pulse.

"'Sup?" I answered, catching Stone's watchful eye. *Intuitive fucker.*

"Arturo's men have Ben."

"Fuck." My eyelids slammed shut. "He alive?"

"Get your ass to the club," Ryker said and hung up.

"Fuck." I shoved my cell in my back pocket.

Ryker hadn't answered my question, but if Ben was dead, Ryker would have said so. That meant he still lived—but I didn't expect for long.

What a fucking mess.

And, I planned on getting the Vipers involved since I wasn't about to sit on my ass and let my best friend lose his life.

"Shaun! Get your ass down here!"

The snap of flip flops announced Shaun's arrival, and I grabbed my keys off the counter. I could feel Stone's focus flitting between us as he stood.

"How ya doin', little girl?" Stone asked, and I shot a scowl over my shoulder.

"Shaun, Stone," I grumbled. "Stone, Shaun."

Shaun's attempted smile wobbled, and she glanced at me, her face pale. "You got news about Dad, didn't you?"

I clipped a quick nod.

She blinked, her eyes hazing with a sheen of tears.

"He's alive," I said, and she gasped, her eyes widening, "but I don't know anything more than that."

A tear slid down her cheek, and I wanted to fold her in my arms, take away all the goddamn pain away. Teeth clenched, I pulled open the garage door and glanced at Stone.

"I'm leaving her in your care."

He nodded. "Good luck."

The squeak of my windshield wipers attempting to keep the pouring rain from hindering my view drove me fucking insane.

So much for the sun-shiny morning.

Hell had taken over the sky, dumping cold buckets and stripping the last of the leaves off the trees. Mother Nature matched my mood—dark and unsettled—but she could never instill the type of fear eating at my gut.

I clenched the steering wheel, hating to have left Shaun even though I trusted Stone to keep her as safe as I could. The haunting fear, the guilt that I'd left her, same as I'd done ten years before cackled between my ears, but I squashed the fucking emotions. Setting aside my responsibility over Shaun came from the need to save her father—not fuck some no-name whore like I'd done the first time around in attempts to get over my desire for my best friend's wife.

The second I hopped out of my truck, the heaven's opened with a vengeance, and I strode to Vigil's office door, shoulders hunched against the soaking, cold rain. Ryker yanked it open at my knock, and I strode into the warm office, dripping all over the wood floor.

"Tell me," I said, simmering as the door slammed shut behind me.

"Sit the fuck down," Vigil said from behind his desk.

I did as told on the chair across from him beside

Devil who tapped away on his laptop, but kept my focus on Ryker.

"They've got him at a stash house in Dorchester."

"He's alive," I said in a rushed exhale.

Ryker nodded. "As of a few minutes ago, but Arturo is on his way."

"How long do we have?"

"What's this *we* shit?" Vigil asked, jerking my attention his way. "The Vipers aren't going to fuck with the goddamn cartel. Last thing we need is a war when we're still trying to build up our ranks after the last one."

I grit my teeth. The last war had been with another club—fifteen years earlier when pot had still been illegal and running it made the outlaw clubs a shit ton of cash.

"I'll go without my colors, and I won't leave anyone breathing," I said, sounding calm as fuck even though I felt anything but.

Vigil stared me down.

"There's only four men on him," Devil said, his focus honed in on his computer screen. "And Arturo's jet won't arrive in Boston until eight-twenty tonight."

"He's out of state?"

"Out of the country," Devil said, still watching his screen.

"Probably took off to keep himself safe while his men attempted to take down Ben," Ryker said.

I turned back to Vigil, hoping for his blessing.

His pale eyes sat cold in his face as he studied me. "Colors off even though your ugly mug will easily tie you to the Vipers if you're caught on any goddamn camera."

"He won't be," Devil muttered, clicking away. "I'll shut everything down."

"I'm going with him," Ryker said, standing.

"The fuck you are." Vigil shot Ryker a glare.

Tension thick enough to strangle a man rose between the two, and I sat back, hating that I needed to wait for their fucking alpha bullshit stare down to end before I could move.

"I got a beef with one of those men," Ryker said, pointing at Devil's laptop, I realized referring to one of the four guarding Ben. "And I plan on looking into his eyes when I rip out his goddamn throat with my *bare fucking hand*."

A shiver slid down my spine. I'd never heard Ryker so calm with deadly intent, and he was one mean mother fucker.

"Get the fuck outta here. Both of you." Vigil

waved us away, muttering curses under his breath. *"And no fucking colors!"*

"My place," I told Ryker, heading once more for the back door. "Half hour. You know what to bring."

"I'll be there, brother."

11

SHAUN

Rain slashed against the cabin's bedroom windows as fear gnawed my stomach raw. I hadn't eaten anything all day—hadn't owned the balls to go downstairs while Drew had worked in the living room rather than his office upstairs.

When Stone had arrived, I'd snuck to the top of the stairs and listened in on their conversation as much as I could make out.

He'd told Stone he didn't want me, and that fuzzy part deep inside wanted to cry. Even telling myself I didn't want *him*—lies, all lies—didn't lessen the hurt his words caused.

Add in the fact Dad got caught, and I curled on the couch in a ball, scared shitless, my stomach a mess, my head pounding like hell.

Stone at least left me alone after tossing me a bottle of over the counter pain-killers.

The clock above the mantle on the far wall clicked loudly along with the falling rain.

My ears strained for any sounds beyond nature, the tick-tock, and my own breathing, and the second the whirl of an engine came clear through the storm, I sat up, my heart thumping hard in my chest, my hands grasping the back of the couch.

The garage door ground open, and I swallowed, my gaze on the door.

Drew came in, his hair wet and clinging to his head. His gaze slid past Stone, who still sat at the table, and landed on me. Anger glinted in his eyes, but the lack of grief gave me hope.

"Dad?" I asked.

Drew strode through the kitchen and living room without answering, taking to the stairs. "Get your bag, Stone," he called.

Stone disappeared outside into the rain before Drew reached the second-floor landing.

I scrambled off the couch and up the stairs, nearly stumbling in my haste. "Drew! What's going on? Is my dad okay?"

He rifled in his closet, and I stood in the bedroom door, wrapping my arms around myself.

"Arturo's men have him."

"Oh God." Fear threatened to buckle my knees, so I locked them tight, needing to focus on something else. "If it weren't for you, none of this would be happening right now." My voice held little conviction, but Drew straightened in his closet door all the same.

"You think I don't fucking know that, Shaun?" he whispered harshly without turning. "You think I haven't been beating up my own ass in my head ever since you two showed up at the Vipers' compound?"

I had nothing to say. No damn sass, no pile of shit to toss at him to make his obvious guilt ten times worse in order to lessen my own. I swallowed hard against the voice tickling the back of my mind, the one calling me a selfish bitch.

"I'll get him back for you, fucking swear it on my goddamn soul."

Resolve settled over me as I cut off that voice, hardening my stance, settling my nerves at his claim. "I'm going with you."

"The fuck you are." Drew tossed a small black bag on his bed. "Sin is coming to stay with you while my other brothers and I go get your dad."

I strode forward, hands fisting at my sides. "But—"

"I have a life to save, and I'm not going to fuck it up this time!" He finally faced me, the guilt in his eyes slamming into me, stealing my breath. "I failed you and your mother. I'm not going to fail your father."

"Drew..."

"I need you as fucking far away from Arturo and his men as possible. Knowing you're here, safe with Sin, I'll be able to focus on doing what needs done."

He cares, holy fuck, he really cares.

It wasn't just about getting pussy for him. He'd meant his goddamn claim on me. My throat tightened as conflicting emotions swarmed through me. Anger came easiest to grasp so I clutched onto it like a life preserver.

I hauled off and slapped him as hard as I could.

He glared.

I scowled back.

"You're going to pay for that," he growled. "After."

"Can't pay me back if you don't *come* back," I tossed out with a sneer, hating that my insides quaked over the fact I'd dared him—*wanted*—him to return to me.

He held my stare, the tension between us thick enough to suck the oxygen from my lungs. A single nod, and he grabbed his bag and stalked out, leaving me alone.

My locked knees gave way, and I sank to the floor, hand clasped over my mouth. Drew had promised to bring my father back to me—but the thought of his not making it out alive himself hurt more than I would have ever expected.

Closing my eyes, I actually offered up a damn prayer, begging whatever god looked down on my pathetic ass would grant me my wish.

12

DREW

Only four fucking men—but Arturo had to know the results of the attempted takeover of the Thode estate. Ben had shot his way out, and I was sure those not swayed by Arturo's money and promises had been put down on the ruthless fuck's command.

I was also sure his men had cleaned the place up spick and span—same as the Vipers would have done to erase evidence of bloodshed.

I stood a block away from the Dorchester stash house, Devil continued to keep on video feed. Ryker awaited at the back for my signal, Stone beside me, all of us connected through earpieces I kept on hand for my business.

Stone and I had promised to take our targets out

of commission with our silenced pistols but not with deadly force—that was Ryker's request to make sure he took the life of the man who had raped his younger sister.

He'd spent years trying to find the fucker, but the rapist had ditched Southie when he'd learned Ryker had put a hit out on him.

Showing back up in the Boston area was a bad decision on that fucker's part, and he would pay for his sins before the night ended, of that, I had no fucking doubt. Poor fucker.

"Two men are still in the front room," Devil's voice came through my earpiece loud and clear. "One in back. The fourth is on the second floor with Thode."

"Ready, Ryker?" I asked, my voice low and steady.

"Say the word." His cold as fuck tone shivered me in my leather jacket.

I started across the street like an everyday Joe Blow, hunched against the rain that continued to fall, Stone at my side. Ryker would go through the back and distract the men watching the front. We just had to keep things quiet so as not to attract unwanted attention from neighbors.

"Now," I told Ryker as we approached the house's walkway.

No smashing in of a door, no shots sounded—but he whispered, "One down," seconds later.

"Devil?" I asked, hurrying up the front stairs.

"Your two are heading Ryker's way," he said in my earpiece.

I kicked in the door. One man hurried away from me back a hallway, and my silencer-muffled shot sent him to the floor with a grunt, his own gun scattering from his hand.

Stone followed on my heels, quietly blowing out the knees of the man on our right at the same time.

Ryker appeared in the doorway directly ahead of me, and I glanced up the stairwell on my left, gun held out in both hands, ready to shoot the fourth fucker.

"Ruiz!" a man hollered from overhead. "The fuck is going on?"

I started up the stairs, noting Ryker in my periphery check out the groaning man I'd shot.

"Remember me, you mother fucking cunt?" Ryker whispered with his death tone, and I knew he'd found the man he wanted.

A stair squeaked beneath me as I started my ascent.

"Ruiz!"

A garbling sounded below from the hallway where Ryker knelt by the soon-to-be dead man, but I didn't take my focus off the top of the stairwell.

Footfalls sounded, and I crouched down—

A quiet pop, and drywall exploded near my head.

I blasted the bloody hand holding the gun sticking around the corner at the top of the stairs, teeth gritted against the man's scream.

Sprinting the last few stairs, I exhaled slowly and rounded the doorway.

Man, meet bullet.

Dark eyes hazed over, and he fell forward, blood oozing from the hole between his eyes.

"Devil?"

"All clear," he told me what I wanted to hear.

I shoved my gun behind my back, stepped over the body at my feet, and hurried to the last door on the right where I'd seen Ben through Devil's computer.

"Fuck." I pulled up short and swallowed back a rush of bile at the sight before me.

The ropes binding him were gone. Ben had been nailed to a goddamn chair, spikes through his wrists and ankles, his head strapped to the back with a metal vise digging into his skin. Fingers littered the bloody floor around him. One eye swelled shut, a gaping hole where the other should have been.

His torso had been sliced to shit, one jagged laceration spilling his guts over his right thigh. They, too, had been cut to shit, irreparable.

His dick and balls had been shorn off and lay between his feet.

"Ben..." I eyed the floor, taking care to step around the blood that would coat my boots and leave more of a mess behind for our cleaners to take care of.

I pulled off one glove, and he didn't twitch as I felt his neck.

A slow pulse fluttered beneath my fingertips. Alive, but barely. If Arturo had hoped to be the one to make the killing blow, he was out of luck. Ben wouldn't survive another hour regardless of care.

"Ben?"

His mouth worked, and I leaned in close. "Sh-sha..."

"Shaun's safe." I swallowed hard.

"Jesus Christ," Stone muttered from behind me. "Fucking *hell*."

"Keep ... safe." Ben slurred his words, blood dribbling down his chin. "Protect. Her."

"I won't let him touch her, I swear to *fucking* God, Ben."

He let out a groan, his mouth working again. "K-kill me. Fucking ... misery."

"Goddamnit, Ben!" I stood. "I can't fucking do that!"

"P-please. Brother."

Throat tight, I stepped back, knowing there was no other option. "Love you, too, brother," I managed to choke out.

Ben's mouth quirked at the corner. "Hug Joanna ... for you." He grimaced, his body trying to fold in on itself as he let out a stomach twisting groan—and I put a bullet between his eyes.

A gurgling, an exhaled breath, and he sagged, lifeless.

Jaw clenched, I backed away, the horror of what lay before my eyes carving deeply into my memory. I'd gifted Ben release from his agony—but I'd sealed my doom with Shaun. She'd hated me before...

Stone clasped my shoulder, and we turned, making our way back downstairs.

Ryker stood over the man in the hallway on the first floor, blood dripping from his hands. A least he'd kept his damn gloves on to rip out the fucker's throat.

"Let's call the cleaners in," I said through clenched teeth, stalking toward the man he'd put down in the living room. He lay unmoving, his throat sliced wide open.

I glanced over at Ryker.

He nodded, sick satisfaction in his cold eyes. "Ben?"

I shook my head.

A flicker of compassion crossed his face. "Sorry, brother."

"Let's make that call and get the fuck out of here the second they show up," I said, knowing I had a worse shit storm ahead of me.

13

—————

SHAUN

Daddy…

D I shot up from bed, my heart pounding as I blinked in the bedroom light I'd left on, never expecting to sleep.

Drew stood in the doorway, barefoot and in sweats, his hair wet as though freshly showered.

I scrambled to sit, my blood seeming to drain from my body at the pain in his eyes. "Dad?" I managed to whisper.

He shook his head.

"No." I stared, denial the wall keeping my emotions in check.

"Shaun." Drew started toward me, and I held up my hand.

"No," I repeated, shaking my head. "No."

The pain in his dark eyes twisted my insides—he wasn't allowed to mourn Dad ... wasn't *allowed* Goddamnit!

A sob caught in my throat, a mere whine escaping as I fought to be the strong woman Dad always wanted me to be.

"I'm so fucking sorry," Drew said, his own voice breaking as he knelt on the bed beside me.

"You told me you would bring him back to me!" I cried, beating against his chest, smacking at the arms he tried to put around me. My walls tumbled to dust and ash. "You promised!" I sobbed.

Tears filled his eyes, but he didn't say a word.

"Fucking liar!" I shrieked, lost to my upheaving emotions.

Drew let me punch him over and over, beating him with ineffectual fists.

Alone.

No mother, no father.

Emptiness, a vast nothing, a vortex of absolute black swirled around my heart and soul as I sobbed, and I wanted to escape its pain.

"Retaliate, you mother fucking asshole!" I shrieked again, beyond desperate.

He didn't.

I smashed my mouth to his and bit his lip—hard enough to draw blood.

Drew groaned, and I crowded closer, the sudden need for him to make me forget overwhelming all else.

"Take it all away," I sobbed against his mouth, kissing and licking, my tears salty against our lips.

"I'm not going to fuck you when you're like this, Shaun."

"Please." I pulled back and peered at him through my tears, my fingers in his beard. "I need you—need to forget."

He cradled my face in his hands and pressed his lips to mine, gentle as fuck, swoon-worthy as hell if I had been in the mood for tenderness.

"Hurt me, damnit," I groaned against his mouth. He continued with his gentle onslaught, but I wasn't having it. Remembering what had pissed him off earlier, I pulled back and slapped him across the face with every ounce of strength I had.

He glared, a low growl rumbling in his chest that set my body on fire even amidst the dripping tears.

I reared back to smack him again, but he caught my wrist. "Is this what you want?" he asked, squeezing my wrist to the point of pain.

"Yes," I whispered, his dominant display exactly

what my heart and body craved.

Drew twisted my arm behind my back and up, taking my shoulder to the point of popping, his black eyes turning feral like a wild animal. "I'll give you what you want, Shaun, but you're not allowed to hate me in the morning."

My breath caught as he spun me and slammed my back against the bed. One yank ripped my panties clean off me, the sting of Drew's other hand in my hair a welcomed distraction.

"I'm going to fuck you so goddamn hard—"

"Yes," I moaned agreement, tilting my head back as he attacked my neck with teeth and tongue while scrambling to rid himself of his sweats.

"Going to fill you so fucking full of my cum, you'll taste it in the back of your throat."

I spread my thighs wider, and he speared into my body with a grunt, my breath catching at the sudden intrusion into my still sore pussy. He didn't give me time to adjust, but rutted into me like an animal, his pelvis slamming against mine with bruising force.

"This what you want?" he asked, stabbing against my cervix and catching my breath.

"God, yes," I sobbed, digging my fingernails into his back and squeezing my thighs tightly around him.

"You want me to hurt you?"

I whimpered, and he grasped hold of my breasts, bringing them together to bite, the stinging pain of his teeth digging into my nipples shooting straight to my clit. My body bowed beneath his, and I clung to him, his grunts and filthy curses about my tight hole, my wet pussy, my perfect fucking tits being all his.

Without a single touch to my clit, I came—hard and long, groaning out his name, my cum gushing around his cock.

"That's it, sweetheart," he growled, his cock on a damn rampage to plunder my insides. "Give it to me."

The second my body came down, he pulled out and flipped me over, shoving my face into the pillow, his fingers tangling in my hair again.

"This ass." He yanked my backside high with one hand while continuing to hold my face down with the other. Teeth dug into my ass cheek, and I gasped as all sorts of live wires shot to life in my head.

"Fucking mine," he whispered with conviction— and I couldn't find it in myself to argue.

I lifted my ass higher, offered it to him on a damn platter, so damn ready for him to take again, that pleadings poured from my lips.

14

DREW

She wanted more—I would fucking give it to her.

I grasped her ass cheeks in my palms and buried my face in her pussy, licking, biting, and sucking, eating her out like a starved man, desperate to forget his miserable existence. My dick throbbed between my legs, but I didn't want to come. Didn't want the high of Shaun to dissipate and leave me swamped in guilt and sorrow.

She'd brought my heart to life after seeing Ben like that … I never wanted it to end.

A deep groan slid past her lips when I shoved my tongue into her puckered hole.

"Goddamn, do you taste good." I bit her ass

cheek again, gnawing my teeth against her satin flesh while rimming her asshole with a fingertip. "So. Fucking. Good."

Shaun whimpered, and I smeared my fingers in the wetness seeping from her pussy, making them good and slick. I pressed against her puckered hole, burying to one knuckle.

"Oh, fuck," she groaned and shoved back toward me as I pushed more. "Holy ... oh God."

I scraped my teeth along her backside, my dick leaking at the thought of burying between her cheeks. She shied away when I shoved another finger in with the first, but she rocked back against my probing fingers a heartbeat later, curses spilling from her lips.

"I'm going to take this ass," I told her, biting hard enough to leave teeth prints.

"Yes."

Fucking music to my ears. I sat up and slid my cock balls deep into her pussy, coating me with her slick arousal. She whimpered again when I pulled out, but I held her cheeks tight around my girth and slid up over her asshole, getting her good and ready for me.

Another dip into her slick pussy, and I held my

dick's head against her puckered hole. Teeth clenched against the desire to shove, I pressed slowly.

"Let me in, sweetheart."

"Oh God, oh God, oh God…" Head to the side and smooshed into the mattress, she bit on her lower lip, her eyes clenched shut as I slipped past the tight ring inside her ass.

Fingers holding her cheeks apart with bruising force, I pulled her back onto my dick.

"Holy fuck!" She shivered and shook, but didn't pull away.

"You're going to take it all," I said through clenched teeth, watching another inch bury inside her tight hole. "I'm going to stretch you out so goddamn good…"

I pulled out to the head and pushed in, burying deeper into her hot body.

"God," she groaned, lifting her ass like a cat in heat.

"Feel good, sweetheart?" I asked, dragging my dick back out.

"Yes, oh, fuck yes." She gulped and whined. "Fucking burns."

I thrust, stuffing her ass full of my dick. "Holy

fucking *Christ*." Eyes closed and head tipped back, I sucked in oxygen through my nose, fighting the tingling in my balls.

Shaun wiggled in my death grip on her ass cheeks. "Please, Drew..." She let out a quiet sob. "Need ... more. Please."

I grasped her hair and yanked her upright, her back against my chest. With my other arm banding around her, I slammed in and upward, stabbing deep into her ass.

"God!" She shrieked, her fingernails digging into my forearm, and I thrust again, slamming her down onto my dick.

"Gonna fill you up with my cum."

"Yes."

I reached between her spread thighs, her clit swollen, her pussy puffy and soaked. "I want you to come all over my hand," I growled while giving her short, jabbing thrusts.

I shoved three fingers deep into her pussy and fucked deep into her ass.

"Drew!" Her head tipped back onto my shoulder, and I bit her neck, the wet sounds of her pussy sucking at my fingers, the scent of sex and her musky sweetness rolling my eyes back into my head.

"Come, Shaun," I managed a harsh whisper and thumbed her clit.

She stiffened in my arms. "Fuck!"

Wetness coated my hand, and I let loose, thrusting like an animal, losing myself in her tight heat as she shuddered in my arms.

"Christ, Shaun—" The first burst of spunk through my dick stole my voice, my thoughts. I pumped every spurt into her body, ripping a grunt from my chest and sending my head on a goddamn high unlike I'd ever known.

My balls ran out, and I held her sweaty body against mine, both of us breathing heavy. She shuddered against me as I gently rubbed my fingers through her cum, gliding along her slit, up and over her clit.

"You're mine, Shaun." I kissed her neck, down her shoulder, my softening dick still buried in her ass. "Every inch." I rimmed the slick hole of her pussy. "Mine to fuck." I dipped a finger inside, and she let out a shuddered breath.

I lifted my hand to her mouth, cracking open an eye. "Mine to protect."

She opened at the brush of my fingertip along her lower lip, and her deep pull on my finger, the swirling of her tongue tasting herself sent another twinge through my balls.

"So fucking perfect," I murmured against her soft as fuck neck.

15

SHAUN

My heart fluttered, and my ears buzzed as I came back down, the tangy taste of my pussy coating my tongue. One last shuddered sigh, and I relaxed against Drew's hard chest, his arms wrapping around me in a protective hold.

A simple yet complex hug.

Reality crashed back into my head, stealing my euphoria.

Tears slid down my cheeks, and I couldn't contain my whimper at the thought of Dad being gone.

"Shh." Drew pulled out of my ass, and I couldn't be bothered by the fact his cum dripped from me. He laid me on my side and kissed my forehead as tears continued to seep from my clenched shut eyelids. "Be right back," he murmured.

I hugged myself, wishing for darkness to consume me so I wouldn't have to deal with the overflow of emotions assaulting me.

Alone.

The word whispered in my head again, and I'd never felt so lost. What the hell would I do with the house? Dad's business? I wasn't even twenty-one yet—would I be allowed access to Dad's bank account in order to even live?

I had a credit card under his name, but how long until that got cut off?

Water ran—the tub, I realized, as Drew left it on and returned a moment later to pick me up and cradle me in his arms. Even though sweat slickened my skin, a chill seemed to seep into my bones, my lungs aching.

He stepped into the tub, and I buried my face in the crook of his neck, his beard soft against my forehead as we sank beneath the hot water, my body slumping against him.

So many damn questions raced through my mind, warring with my grief, and overwhelming me with details I had no clue how to deal with.

I wanted to cling to Drew and never let go, but it

was wrong to like him. Want him. I couldn't help myself. Drew made me feel like I was important, he offered comfort willingly. He'd broken down my walls, and I couldn't decide if I wanted to hate him or fall harder.

My ass burned. My thighs hurt from being spread so damn wide. My pussy ached from his taking in so short a time. It'd been fucking glorious, divine. Delicious. But, it'd ended, leaving me once more empty inside, questioning everything.

"Tell me what happened," I whispered, needing to get out of my damn head.

"We were too late." His voice cut off abruptly, and I waited as he swallowed a few times. "There's nothing I could have done," he whispered, his voice ragged.

Recognizing guilt came easy for me. So much more than grief coated his words. "It's not your fault. Dad shouldn't have gone on his own. It's his mistake —his fault—not yours," I whispered through my tears.

Drew didn't speak for a time, and I laid against him, wishing for a mom's advice, wishing for a father's blessing over my feelings for a badass biker as he lifted handfuls of water to trickle down my shoulder.

"So, what happens now?" I asked, my voice loud in the still bathroom.

"I promised your dad I would look after you," he said a short time later. "I promised to protect you."

Mine to protect, he'd vowed while slipping his cum-covered finger between my lips.

Because my father had given the responsibility of me away like a birthday present or some such shit before heading off to certain death.

I frowned, that fact whispering through my head a second time, and I pulled away from Drew's hold.

"Hey."

Climbing out of the tub, I didn't turn toward him, didn't acknowledge he wanted my attention. I grabbed a towel from the rack and started to dry off quickly, wanting space. Needing it.

A damn war boomed in my head, raging with almost irrational thoughts.

"Shaun." The water started to drain, and I watched in my periphery as he grabbed the other towel.

"Dad's dead," I stated, hating that my throat clogged again, "so you no longer need to look after me."

"You're mine," he said, tucking the towel around his waist.

I spun to face him fully, hanging onto the pissiness in my head, keeping more tears at bay, the hard rock-like feeling in my stomach over his goddamn assumptions.

"I don't *belong* to you, Drew. I'm not some possession, a gift from my dad that you get to do with as you wish. I am a grown-ass woman, more than capable of taking care of myself."

He let out a heavy sigh, his shoulders slouched. "I'm tired as fuck, Shaun, and I don't want to do this right now. Can we talk in the morning?"

"Fine," I snipped. "But, I'm sleeping on the couch." I spun and returned to the bedroom, grabbing up the clothes I'd taken off before climbing into Drew's bed hours earlier.

He didn't argue as I stomped down the stairs. He didn't follow after me. Didn't demand I return to his bed.

Preferring it that way—or so I told myself—I eyed the couch, remembering too late I hadn't brought a pillow down with me. "No biggie," I muttered to myself. "Not like I'm going to sleep anyway."

Two hours later, darkness still ruled the night, and anger reigned over my head, keeping my grief buried. To Drew, I was a responsibility, probably penance for his past failures to my family—but good for him, I came with a willing pussy. Something to play with—protect according to him—he probably just said that to keep me close to lessen his guilt over Mom.

Well, I was no man's toy. No man's possession, either.

Without either parent, it was up to me to live my own life. Freedom to choose, freedom to head into my future, and hopefully make something of it other than being a rich woman whose father's name gave her respect, even if it was with the wrong crowds.

Real freedom had come at a heavy cost, one I couldn't stand to think on, and as my anger began to fade, my sorrow returned. I climbed off the couch and crept back upstairs.

Drew's light snores met my ears as I eased his bedroom door closed without lingering for one last look at his sprawled form.

I shut myself in his office and rang Krystal. She didn't answer. I rang again.

"Who the fuck are you, and what the hell do you want?" she said, her voice groggy and pissed. "It's three in the goddamn morning!"

"It's me," I whispered, my hand over my mouth and the receiver.

"Shit!" The phone crackled in my ear, and I imagined her jerking upright to sit. "Shaun! Where the fuck are you?"

I shot off the address on the electric bill in front of me. "I need to get the hell outta here. Can you come get me? Please, Krystal."

"Topsfield—it'll take me about forty or so minutes."

"That's fine. Don't speed. Just get here safe. My baby sitter is passed out cold, so no honking the horn when you pull up the driveway."

"You got it."

I hung up and wrote a quick note before slipping back downstairs and shoving my feet into the whore's flip flops.

My clothes from the club and my Jimmy Choos lay up in Drew's bedroom still, but I wasn't about to chance his waking up. Besides, I had a shit-ton of clothes at Krystal's and my apartment, and even more back home at Dad's house.

My house.

Throat tight, I sat on the couch and hugged my legs to my chest to await my ride that would free me once and for all.

DREW

My eyelids jerked open—*too damn quiet*. I rolled out of bed, that goddamn feeling of something bad settling over my brain as I crept down the stairs.

No Shaun.

"Shaun?" I called, hurrying back up the stairs.

The office and bathroom doors stood open. Empty.

"Shaun!" I hollered, knowing silence would meet my ears. "Goddamnit!"

I searched for my cell and found it on the counter, where I'd tossed it after getting back the night before. I'd missed the notification ding that a car drove up the driveway. I clicked on the App and watched as a blue BMW came to life in the house's floodlights.

Shaun snuck out the door and rushed to climb in.

"Fuck." I scrolled. Zoomed in.

Brow furrowed, I studied the blonde woman driving but didn't have a fucking clue who she was. I scrolled down a bit more and repeated the license plate to myself.

Shaun had made a call…

I checked my cell and found none outgoing since I'd called the cleaners to clean up our mess, so headed for the stairs.

A folded note lay on my desk beside the landline phone she must have used.

My stomach twisted as I grabbed the piece of paper and unfolded it.

I'm not interested in being "yours" because you feel obligated to my dad. Please stay away from me and let me live my own life.

My jaw clenched. Shaun had no fucking clue the danger she was in.

I should have forced the conversation we'd needed

to have the night before. Shaun needed to understand that just because her father was gone didn't mean Arturo would no longer be a threat. Especially once he found his four men and Ben's body gone from the house —if he hadn't already. Zero trace they'd ever been there. He'd want blood. Bodies piled up in revenge.

I prayed like fuck he'd never learn it was the Vipers who'd come for Ben and dished out what was coming to those fuckers.

Cursing under my breath, I hit *69 on my phone and jotted down the number. I didn't expect anyone to answer, but I called anyway. Twice. An automated voice told me the owner of that number wasn't available at the moment.

I rang Devil.

"Too fucking early, Drew."

"I need an address."

He heaved a heavy exhale. "Kinda busy at the moment."

"Tell the whore to get off your dick," I shot, striding into my bedroom. "Now."

"Fucker."

"Now, Devil!"

"Shit, man," he grumbled, but I could hear muffled movement. "Calm the fuck down."

"Shaun took off in a blue BMW."

"Fuck."

"Yeah."

"Hold on a sec."

I yanked on a pair of jeans and socks, my cell between my shoulder and ear.

"Okay ... whatcha got?"

I rattled off the plate number and grabbed a t-shirt out of a drawer.

Once I had Devil on speaker, I listened to computer keys clicking while I finished getting dressed.

"It's registered to a Krystal Davis. 17 Baker Street, apartment 1B."

"Thanks." I hit end and dialed Stone.

While hurrying downstairs for my boots and keys, I filled him in. "Will you go with me? Just in case?"

"Give me ten, and I'll be ready to go," he said, the music from his dojo's early morning kickboxing class muffled in the background.

"Thanks, brother," I said, scooting out into the garage, my gut in fucking knots over the thought Arturo could have gotten to Shaun already.

Teeth not brushed, no coffee in my stomach, but I strode out my door, not giving a shit. My woman had taken off, and the thought I might have lost her trumped all else. Finding her was my focus. Nothing else mattered.

I made a quick call to Vigil to tell him what had gone down—including the shit from the night before.

"Need me to bring back up?" he asked as I pulled into Stone's parking lot, and I breathed a sigh of relief he focused on that rather than our possibly having started a war.

"Stone and I are gonna go in quiet, but I'll be in touch."

"Anything you need, brother."

"Appreciate that, Vigil." I put my truck into park, my gaze snagging on the to-go cup Stone carried in one hand.

He handed it over while climbing into the cab.

"I could fucking kiss you," I muttered, taking the offered mug.

Stone snorted and slammed the door shut. "Not my type, fucker."

I took a quick swallow of coffee and peeled out of the parking lot.

We drove in silence, every second that ticked by heightening my blood pressure. If Arturo got to Shaun before I did ... if he fucking hurt her...

"I'll fucking kill him," I muttered, my stare on the

highway, my thoughts a million times darker than the overcast sky. I tossed my cell to Stone. "Try the one-seven-eight-seven number—it's Krystal's, Shaun's friend."

"Want me to leave a message?" he asked as it continued to ring without anyone picking up.

"Put it on speaker."

The last ring came through loud in the cab, the automated voice annoying as fuck.

"Krystal—this is Drew," I said after the beep. "I'm a friend of Shaun's father, and I need you to call me back as soon as possible."

Stone hung up, and I clenched the steering wheel until my knuckles ached.

I pulled up a block away from the address Devil had given me, and we scoped the road, the front of the apartment building, and the few cars parked on the street.

"What's the plan?" Stone asked, his focus turning on me.

"We're going in." I shut off the truck and climbed out into the drizzle, checking my gun tucked into the back of my jeans.

Shoulders tense and senses on high fucking alert, I stalked toward the building, eyes scanning, shoulders hunched inside my leather jacket. I scowled over the lack of a buzzer in the entryway to Shaun's building.

My lips pressed tight as I waltzed on in like I owned the damn place. 1B sat at the end of the short hallway. I knocked, and no one answered. I eased the door handle, but it didn't give.

"Try her again," I told Stone, who stood on my right.

Ear pressed to the door, I held my breath and listened, the muffled ringing from my cell in Stone's hand the only sound other than music from the neighbors across the hall. No footsteps, no ringtone came through Shaun's door.

The knife-like feeling twisting in my gut worsened. "Goddamnit."

I nodded toward the building's front, and we strode back outside. The rain had picked up, and until we circled around the building to the apartment's slider door, drips fell off the end of my nose. They never locked the fucking slider—or someone had already broken in.

I slipped inside, scanning the living area on autopilot, my gun held in front of me, ready to pop a fucker in the face. Stone's footfalls whispered away to my left as I made my way toward a dark hallway.

"Clear," he whispered, and I moved with stealth,

lethal intent, gaze flitting from one opened door to the other ahead of me.

I took the room on the right, whipping around the corner, gun at the ready.

Nothing.

"Clear," I whispered, Stone's echo from the room across the hall coming a heartbeat later.

The bathroom lay straight ahead, and a quick glance inside showed it empty as well. But, Shaun had been there. The leggings and t-shirt she'd snatched up off the floor before hightailing it downstairs the evening before, sat on top of the hamper basket.

I shoved my gun away, my brow dented so damn hard my head hurt. "Where the fuck are they? Cell."

Stone handed it over without a word, and I tried Krystal's number—again.

"Fuck." I hit end when it went straight to voicemail. I dialed Devil.

"Can you get eyes on Arturo's estate again?" I asked when he answered, striding back to the bedroom I'd cleared.

"Give me a few."

I flicked on the overhead light and took a better look, hands on my hips. Gray and blue bedspread and curtains—nothing pink with unicorns or girly frills anywhere. My lips twitched.

So different from her mom.

A picture sat on her bed stand, and I picked it up, flipping it over even though I knew what I'd find.

The same picture had sat on her bed stand when she'd been a kid back at Ben's house.

My throat thickened as my focus went directly to the little girl in Joanna's arms rather than her parents. The sparkling eyes, the missing two front teeth, the hair blowing in the wind from the ocean behind them, a melting ice cream cone in her hand...

I had taken that picture, I remembered, while rubbing my thumb over her image—on Shaun's sixth birthday.

"Arturo's there," Devil said in my ear, pulling me back to the present.

I set the picture back down.

"Shaun?" I asked and held my breath.

My lungs ached by the time he finally fucking answered. "No."

I sucked in oxygen. "Nothing?"

"No trace of any woman from what I can see other than his wife—and she's sporting a nice black eye. Think he found out she was having an affair with Thode?"

My brow furrowed again. "Don't know. Don't care. She made that goddamn bed, she can sleep in it. Thanks, brother."

I hung up, wondering if Arturo had rooms without cameras and met Stone's gaze.

"Now what?" he asked.

Fuck, if I knew—but I wasn't about to stop looking. Going to the kingpin's house was out of the goddamn question. "We're going through their shit. See if we can't find out where or who they hang out with—and pray like fuck we find them with friends."

With a quick nod, Stone left me alone in Shaun's room.

17

SHAUN

Rather than sleep, I talked Krystal into packing a bag and hightailing it away from our apartment for a little while. I knew Drew would come looking for me, and I didn't want to be anywhere he might think to look—and find me.

He'd called her cell and left a message, but we ignored his request.

Feeling the need to splurge, relax, and just fucking live in silence for a few days, I pulled money from an ATM off Dad's credit card, and got us a suite at the Boston Harbor Hotel. We'd be skipping classes, but at that point, I didn't give two shits. I needed to relax.

We ate a late breakfast and drove around downtown doing a little shopping while wasting time until check-in even though rain fell.

I told her everything that happened from the moment I'd been torn from her side on Friday night. She had been worried sick, and wanted to call the cops but knew better considering who my father was.

"Seriously, I thought you were dead," she muttered as we sat at a red light Boston's traffic creeping along in front of us. "And here you were getting fucked out of your mind by an asshole biker."

My pussy twinged at the memory even though soreness lingered between my thighs. I sighed and tipped my head back against the seat, closing my eyes. "I'm so damn tired. Miss my dad—miss the old normal even though I didn't have any freedom." My throat tightened. "I'd give anything to go back to the way things were."

Krystal grasped my hand. "My dad will help you figure all the legal shit out when you're ready, once you have answers."

Drew hadn't told me shit about what went down when he'd gone for Dad—but it couldn't have been good from the level of exhaustion he'd shown over my pissiness, refusing to fight. I hadn't thought to ask

Drew about Dad's body—or what Drew and his biker brothers had done with it. Knowing Dad's lifestyle, having met a few of the Vipers, I wondered if I would even get a chance for a final goodbye. A lowering of a dark box into black earth, void of color and light...

I swallowed hard, tears stinging my clenched eyes.

So many unanswered questions, but I had no interest in calling Drew for details or having that little talk he'd wanted to take care of in the morning. Going to the cops was not an option. No matter how heartbroken or pissy, I wouldn't put myself on the wrong side of the Vipers.

I needed quiet, time to grieve, time to come to terms with the future of freedom, one I wouldn't be able to share with either parent.

"It's gonna be okay, Krystal," I whispered as the hotel came into view, but more for my benefit than hers. "It's gonna be okay."

Once we settled into our suite, we turned her phone back on and got online, snooping every news site we could find, hoping for a write up about a shootout, a massacre, drive-by—whatever had taken place between the cartel and Vipers.

Nothing. Not a hint, no breaking stories of a gunfight with casualties.

"You really should go to the police," Krystal said, powering off and tossing her cell aside.

"And tell them what, exactly?" I asked, same as the first time she'd suggested it, and flopped onto the king-sized bed beside her. "That my dad was a major kingpin here in Boston? That he worked for one of the most-wanted cartel leaders?" I snorted. "They'll seize it all, Krystal. I'll have *nothing* to go with my no one."

"Well, I think that after our time here, we ought to go see my dad. Tell him everything. He'll know what to do."

I let out a heavy sigh. "Okay."

We laid in silence, and I sniffed back the few tears leaking down my cheeks.

"What time is our spa treatment?" Krystal asked, and I turned my head to check the alarm clock. "Half hour."

She hopped up and grabbed a bottle we'd brought along out of the mini-fridge, the cheap kind with a screw lid for easy removal. "Wine time."

"Sounds good to me."

Our plastic cups clicked together on a toast a few minutes later. "To our futures," she murmured, her hazel eyes staring me down as though tempting me to disagree.

"To our futures." I sipped, eyes closing at the dry red slipping down my throat.

I couldn't imagine anything but a bleak one— but at least I lived and had that damn freedom I'd always longed for.

It just came at a shitty fucking price.

———

The spa helped relax me, but nothing eased my grief. I knew it would take time—a long fucking time —but I would get through it. It had taken ten years for me to be able to think about Mom without crying. A few days, a few answers, and putting things in order would give me something else to focus on rather than my lack of family.

But, how would I prove Dad was even dead without a body? Report him missing? How would I get my hands on the money once I even took that step? Dad had a safe at home, but I had no clue how to get into it.

God.

"We need more alcohol," Krystal muttered.

I rolled my head along the back of the love seat. "Wanna go out?"

"Catch an Uber to Benny's?"

Drew didn't know Krystal other than grabbing her number off his phone I'd used, so he wouldn't know to look for us at her cousin's club. The thought of getting drunk and forgetting sounded like a damn good idea. "Let's go."

We didn't have clubbing clothes, but I didn't give a shit. Jeans and a t-shirt would work just fine. It wasn't like I wanted to find some guy for a random hook-up. After having been ruined by Drew for a dick other than his own, goddamn him, trying another didn't appeal.

Krystal never left home without her makeup and hair shit, so I was at least able to cover the bags under my eyes and make my long hair presentable.

She called Benny to let him know we were coming in, and he promised to meet us at the side door again whenever we texted him to let him know we arrived.

"Shit, that man has tried calling you like twenty times!" Krystal said after hanging up with her cousin and scrolling through her phone.

"Relentless mother fucker," I muttered, snatching up my sneakers, the truth of those words slamming into my head. He'd loved my mother once upon a time ... did the sicko think of her when he'd been between my thighs? Had he imagined having the woman he'd given up to my dad beneath him rather than little old me?

My mouth watered as nausea stirred.

The sick fuck. I'd been right to leave—and Krystal had done right to not call him back like he'd asked in the message from hours earlier.

Krystal let out a huff and powered her phone back off. "You'd think he'd get the damn hint and leave you the fuck alone."

I grunted my agreement while lacing up a sneaker.

A knock sounded on our door, and we both paused in putting our second shoes on. My heart thumped heavy, and I glanced at Krystal, my face furrowing into a scowl. She raised a brow and stood, hurrying to the door to peer out the peephole, one shoe trailing laces behind her.

"Yeah?" she called out as I moved to her side, my adrenaline racing.

I took a quick peek out the hole—a man in a suit, a tray in hand. Not Drew, thank fuck.

"I have complimentary wine and a cheese tray," the guy said, glancing at a paper he lifted closer to his face, "for a Shaun Thode."

"No one I recognize," I whispered to Krystal.

"Huh. Must be a room warming gift." She grinned. "Free wine and cheese? Yes, please."

Two minutes later, the server was out the door with a ten dollar tip, and Krystal tapped her plastic cup to mine while popping a piece of cheese into her mouth.

"To free vino!" she said around the cheese.

We drank, kicked back off our sneakers, and devoured the cheese, crackers, and fruit on the plate rather than head out to Benny's right away. I found my vision going fuzzy as the last of my wine slid down my throat.

"I think I drank too much," I said with a laugh.

Krystal tipped her head back on the couch, her eyes closing. "You and me both. That was some potent shit."

I picked up the empty bottle, trying to focus on the label. "Old vintage." I squinted, but my fucking eyes crossed. "Wonder what percent," I slurred, and the bottle dropped to the floor.

I waved my hand in front of my face, rubbed my fingertips together.

Numb.

"Huh. Weird."

My eyes closed, and I felt myself slip off the couch—I didn't feel my body hit the floor.

———

Cigars.

Body odor.

Cinnamon rolls?

I cracked an eyelid open, my memory toast. My head pounded—thank fuck no sunlight streamed through a window to blind me. Pushing up to sit throbbed my head, and I grasped my temples, groaning.

Too much wine.

"God." I lifted my head, squinting while glancing around.

Small room. Gray walls.

No Krystal, and I wasn't sitting in the hotel room.

"What the fuck?" My heartbeat tripled, and I swallowed back a bout of nausea.

No windows—one door.

I stumbled across the small room, the door handle cold beneath my trembling hand, but it didn't give when I twisted.

I pounded on the door. "Hey!" My scream echoed in the empty room, and tightness in my chest threatened to double me over. "Hello!" I hollered again, my voice catching on a sob. "Krystal?"

No one answered, and the door remained unopened and locked, shutting me in.

Where the hell am I, and how the fuck did I get here?

Thoughts of sex slaving and skin sales I'd heard whispers of slithered through my brain, shivering me with goosebumps. Bile stung the back of my throat again. I sat on the bed and hugged my knees, my gaze locked on the door, not bothering to try to be strong.

Tears rolled down my face and whimpers escaped my lips.

I wanted answers—yet I didn't want to hear the truth of my future.

Was Krystal taken, too? Was she locked up in another room, scared shitless over thinking we might end up a slave to some sexual sicko intent on breaking our spirits and having us crawl around on all fours? What if the fucker was into whips and chains? Blood and scat play?

Shuddering, I squeezed myself tight, wishing for arms stronger than my own as my eyelids slid shut.

Never should have left Drew—

The door snicked open, jolting my eyelids back up. My breath caught as a huge, scary as fuck guy entered and stepped to the side. His stare sent another shiver over me.

I opened my mouth to spew questions, but another body filled the doorway, and my words clogged in my throat.

Dark eyes. Black hair slicked back. A scar on the corner of his mouth twisted his lips in a sneer.

Him.

The blood drained from my face, leaving me lightheaded.

"Hello, princess."

His smile twisted my stomach.

Arturo.

18

DREW

We didn't find a damn thing, not a goddamn thing to point where Shaun might have gone. We ransacked the apartment and came up empty.

Devil had gotten us both girls' schedules, but we stuck around campus for two classes—neither showed. They could have been at a friend's house for all we knew, watching chick flicks and eating ice cream.

Shaun had to know I'd come after her, so she'd be lying low someplace. While a brat, she was smart enough to hide where I wouldn't think to look. That meant she'd avoid her family home—fuck knew what that place even looked like or if Arturo cleaned up the mess his men had made in their attempts to exact revenge on Ben for killing one of the cartel's own all those years ago.

I wondered if the cops had gotten involved. If so, they'd be swarming the Thode estate, looking for Shaun, most likely.

I scrubbed a hand over my face and tossed the girls' bills back onto the kitchen table. We'd returned to their apartment hoping they'd done the same, but no such fucking luck.

"Stone!" I hollered.

"Yeah?" He appeared in the doorway.

"We're wasting time. Let's head back to the club," I said, pushing back my chair. "See what Devil can stir up."

My stomach in all kinds of knots, we headed back to the club. Every minute felt like a fucking hour. Krystal's cell remained shut off, every one of the calls I made went straight through to her voice mail.

I finally left another message, telling her Shaun's life was in danger—and not from me. Begging wasn't my thing, but I didn't hold back, my damn voice catching on the last "please".

I wanted to down a bottle of JD but needed to be on point, alert, and ready to go for when we found her.

Devil tracked down Krystal's parents, and a feigned sales call put through that night asking for her ended with a, "She's not home right now" answer before I hung up. He also made a connection to the Benny kid who recently opened a club up downtown, and I made that call on speakerphone for my brothers in Vigil's office, praying like fuck we'd have a breakthrough.

"The fuck you want with my cousin?" Benny asked when I asked if he'd seen Krystal or Shaun.

"Shaun's father put her in my care," I said, wanting to spew every goddamn truth to the idiot not wanting to answer questions, but not knowing him from Adam, I had to tread carefully. "Her father went missing, and Shaun took off this morning. You know who her father is?"

"Who doesn't? But, not my monkey—"

"It's a life or death situation," I shot out, my voice snippy as fuck, revealing the anger and unrest shredding my insides. "Shaun's life is in the balance—so that means Krystal's very well could be, too, if they're together."

"You fucking with me?" Benny said, his voice less certain.

I gripped my cell tighter, my focus on the seconds of our call ticking by. Seconds that could be the difference between life and death. "I wouldn't fuck around with something like this."

"Krystal called a few hours ago asking me to let her and Shaun into the club tonight."

"They didn't show up," I stated, my eyes closing briefly as everything inside me stilled.

"No, but Krystal is always late as fuck. They're probably doing girl things—makeup and all that shit."

They could have been, but my gut told me otherwise. Especially since it was after eleven.

"Did she say where they were?" I asked, glancing over at Vigil to see his lips flatten into a thin line.

"No, but I could tell she already had a drink or two in her. Fucking lightweight... Fuck. You don't think—"

"Yeah, I do."

"Fuck, man. Shouldn't we call the cops or some such shit?"

Arturo's place, I mouthed to Devil sitting at Vigil's desk across the office from me. "No cops," I told Benny. "Not yet. I've got a lead I'm going to jump on. I'll be in touch."

We hung up a second later, and I hopped off the couch, peering over Devil's shoulder as his hands flew over his keyboard.

Video feeds sprang to life in little squares across his screen. My attention flitted from one to the next, but no Shaun.

"Fuck." I scrubbed a hand down over my face and beard, giving it a frustrated tug. "Can't find Krystal's cell if it's turned off, right?" I asked Devil.

He shook his head.

"See if she has OnStar?"

"She doesn't."

"Fuck." Hands tied—sucked ass. I met Vigil's stare. "She's mine, Vigil. I'm fucking claiming her— and I'm asking for my brothers' help."

"You eat anything today?" he asked rather than acknowledge my request, and I shook my head. "Go get something in the kitchen. Now. Devil and I will keep on it."

I let out a held breath and nodded. "Thank you."

Pushing out of his office into the club's main room, I felt a hell of a lot better. A handful of brothers hung out, shooting the shit and pool, but I couldn't be bothered to acknowledge them with how my head spun.

Tina approached me, but I held up a hand, scowling, stopping her in her tracks.

The Vipers had a big commercial-like kitchen behind the bar, but we didn't keep a cook or any such shit. If a brother felt like cooking, he did. If one of the old ladies or whores was in the mood to put out a spread, they did.

My stomach churned at the thought of food, but Vigil was right. I needed to eat. The fridge had half a box of leftover pizza on the bottom shelf. I ripped off the sticky note naming it Greed's, plunked my ass on a stool by the island, and chowed down cold mushroom pizza.

A beer or ten would have gone down really fucking well, but...

I needed to punch something. Hard. Adrenaline had been rushing through my veins on and off all goddamn day, and I couldn't keep my knee from bouncing.

Ryker came through the door as I crammed the second slice between my lips.

"You heard?" I asked around a mouthful.

He nodded, his brow furrowed. "It's why I came in. I put out some feelers with a few old friends."

"Appreciate it. I claimed her, so you don't need to worry about Vigil getting all over your ass for helping me."

"Good." Sitting, he let out a heavy exhale, something I'd never heard him do.

"You okay?" I asked, pushing the pizza box toward him.

"Yeah." He grabbed the last piece. "Finally got my fucking revenge, but to be honest, I do not feel as satisfied as I'd hoped."

"How's your sister, anyway?"

He shrugged. "A basket case when she isn't drunk off her ass."

"Sorry, brother."

"Shit happens. The cleaners did a job on Arturo's place. Unless he goes in there with crime scene swabs between floorboards, he won't find jack shit."

I nodded and swallowed my last bite of pizza. "What'd they do with the bodies?"

"Cut up Arturo's men and fed them to the fishes out in the ocean."

"Ben's body?"

"They put it on ice—waiting to see what you wanted to do since you didn't give them an order."

I cursed under my breath. Yet another piece of shit I had to deal with. Shaun would want closure—she'd probably need it in order to get her inheritance. While I didn't understand all the legal bullshit, I knew a body would be better than no body—no matter its shape.

But, a bullet from my gun lay inside his goddamn brain somewhere.

"Fuck."

Ryker clasped my shoulder and squeezed. "We're gonna find her, Ward. I fucking promise."

I nodded, remembering all the promises I'd made over the previous couple of days. They hadn't meant jack shit.

———

My cell rang, jerking me awake. Neck stiff from stretching on the too-small couch in Vigil's office, I sat up with a grimace and grabbed my cell off the small table beside me.

Krystal.

Heart speeding, I swiped to answer. "Krystal, is Shaun with you?"

"No." Her voice caught on a sob, her voice pitched high as hell.

"Fuck." I hopped up, hand going straight for my hair as I glanced at the clock on the wall. Four in the morning. "Where the fuck are you? What happened?"

"W-we got a room at the Boston Harbor Hotel." Her sniffle and whimper clenched my teeth.

"Someone brought us a cheese plate and wine—I-I think it had something in it that knocked us both out."

"Shaun?"

"She was gone when I woke up less than a minute ago. H-her sneakers are still here."

Goddamnit all to fucking hell.

"Did you recognize the guy?" I asked, my voice hard as steel as I strode across the office and to yank open the door into the club. "Did he say anything to you?"

"N-no. He just said it was a complimentary snack." She let out another whine-like wail. "We didn't think anything of it."

"Shit." Seeing the club empty, I slumped back on the couch, squeezing the bridge of my nose between two fingers.

"I'm so sorry," Krystal sobbed. "So fucking sorry. I shoulda called. Shoulda made her call you back."

"Not your fault." I clenched my teeth for a second, fighting for calm. "Call your cousin Benny— he was worried last night when you didn't show up. And I'll let you know when I find her."

Because I would. Or I'd die trying.

A half-hour later, Vigil, his brother Ranger our acting VP, along with Devil, Stone, and Ryker, sat around the office, a heavy silence over us. Devil's fingers clicking on his keyboard was the only sound other than my heartbeat thrumming in my ears.

"He has her."

I hopped off the couch and crowded close at his back, my focus landing on his screen.

Shaun lay on a bed, curled on her side.

I stared, my heart in my goddamn throat. "Zoom in?"

Devil did, and I watched—waited—for her chest to move. A rush of air left me as she breathed.

"Mother fucking asshole," I hissed, fists clenching.

"Can't take on the goddamn cartel," Vigil said, knowing I thought of going in, guns blazing.

"The fuck we can't," I countered, scowling over Devil's head and across the desk.

Vigil's stare didn't waver as he tapped a finger on his desk in steady rhythm. "We're going to find another way."

"What?" I shot out, so damn ready to roll, my legs shook.

"Devil?" Vigil turned his focus on our tech man. "I've told you to get shit on every goddamn politician and law enforcement agent in our area, but what about this prick?"

Devil let out a sarcastic huff through his nose. "Please."

"You've got a couple hours to dig up more shit—enough that bastard is willing to give Shaun back in exchange for our silence."

"He won't agree," I said, and I noted Ryker's nod of agreement in my periphery.

"Everyone has their price," Ranger said, drawing my focus off his brother. Ricky "Ranger" Capello was only a year younger than Vigil, and if one didn't know better, they might think the two men were twins. But that's where the similarities ended. Ranger might be rough with his fists and words, but the man was a goddamn soft fucker inside.

He'd also know about everyone having a price. The man had paid a high one once upon a time.

"And what happens when Arturo decides he's had enough and comes for the entire fucking club?" I asked, turning my focus back on Vigil.

"We'll deal with the fucker if it comes to that." Vigil leaned forward, elbows on his desk, his stare intent on my face. "But for now, we're going to focus on getting what we need—to get your woman back."

My throat tightened, and I dipped my head in a single nod. "Thank you."

"Get to work, Devil," Vigil barked. "We're only

going in five strong to keep Arturo's panties from twisting, so you'd better prepare your asses. Devil will stay here, our ace in the hole. Our fucking protection." As one, we all moved from our spots. "And no fucking booze!" Vigil's holler followed us out the door.

19

SHAUN

Arturo squatted beside my bed, zero fear over the fact I might haul off and kick him in the face. He smiled up at me, his grotesque scar turning my stomach. "I've been looking for you."

I kept my lips sealed against the sob and rising nausea wanting to spew sour wine all over him.

"Little princess." His gaze roamed slowly down my face, lingering on my lips. "Where's your father?"

"Dead," I spit out, sudden anger sitting me upright.

His brow furrowed for a split second as his gaze shot back up to my eyes. "Is he, now?"

My heart stalled out—he didn't know—which meant he had no clue where I'd been, who'd I'd been with, and what the Vipers had done.

"W-well, he never came back for me," I managed, my voice shaky as hell as my heartbeat raced.

"And where did he whisk you off to?"

I swallowed, needing to force words out. "S-safe house."

"Bullshit," Arturo snipped, rising to his feet to loom over me. "I know every goddamn thing about your father—shit even he didn't know himself. Where were you?"

Knowing the man Arturo was, what he was capable of, I wasn't about to give him the truth, any reason to exact further revenge.

I clamped my lips shut.

Arturo studied me in silence, and my mind went crazy with all the ways he might end me, end the Thode bloodline—or sell me as a sex slave.

Suddenly aware of my full bladder, I squeezed my thighs together with a whimper.

"He was fucking my wife," Arturo said, his tone more conversational. "The fucker thought he could find an in. My men had him trussed up good for me, but what do I find when I arrive in Boston? Nothing. An empty, clean as fuck stash house. No men, no Benjamin Thode tied up tight awaiting my judgment. So, I'll ask again." His voice hardened. "*Where did he hide you away?*"

I clenched my eyes shut, digging for the strength Dad always encouraged me to grasp hold of. "I told you."

"And I'm calling bullshit. He wouldn't leave his little princess alone, but he also didn't trust anyone."

Anger began to simmer inside me, and I clung to that emotion like a damn lifeline. "He made the mistake of trusting the men you snuck into his ranks," I shot back, my voice steadier than I'd expected.

"I couldn't get to the two of you, though. Loyal as fuck, but that Drew guy had failed him all those years ago when my cousin got shot—I knew your shadows would eventually, too."

The blood rushed from my face, my mouth dried in a second flat.

Arturo's gaze narrowed, and I fought to keep my face passive as he studied me. "*That's* where you were."

I didn't twitch an eye, but goddamnit, I gulped.

"He sent you to the Vipers. They're who took out my men. Took your father."

"My father's dead," I whispered, unable to help myself. "You've had your revenge. Please let me go."

"They're sneaky fuckers," Arturo went on as though I hadn't said a word. "They have the means to cover their asses." He turned toward the man beside the door. "Round up the boys. It's time to pay our local motorcycle club a little visit."

The guard disappeared, and Arturo turned back toward me. He leaned onto the bed with his fists, caging me between his arms, his coffee-laced breath fanning my face.

Bile burned the back of my throat, and I closed my eyes, turning my head.

Arturo grasped my chin and jerked my face back toward him. "Look at me."

Whimpering, I obeyed, hating my weakness, hating the hopelessness eating away at my mind.

"I'd planned on watching you bleed out, but maybe..."

I shrank into myself, terrorized by the look in his dark eyes.

He grinned, but the lust shining in his eyes didn't lessen. "My lying, cheating, whore of a wife is taking a very long vacation. I could use someone to warm my bed."

"The fuck I will," I shot out, that anger simmering to life again, thank fuck. "You try, and I'll cut your dick off the first chance I get."

He chuckled and trailed his knuckles along my cheek, sending a shiver through me, waking the body trembles again. "It's only fitting. Your father used my wife, I use you." He grasped my chin again as I tried to back away from him, his fingers digging into my soft flesh enough to bruise.

"Don't," I bit out the word.

"Don't what?" Arturo's gaze dropped to my lips again. "You're mine now, Shaun, and I can do whatever the fuck I want with you." He leaned in, and I clenched my lips and eyelids shut.

"I can tie you up. Lick you from head to toe. Eat your young pussy and ass. Take every goddamn hole in your body—and you won't be able to stop me."

I winced as his fingers bruised my jaw.

"I sometimes like to share, too," Arturo went on. "Would you like that, Princess? One of my guards shoving his dick into your ass while I'm buried deep inside your tight pussy, another feeding you his until you can't breathe?"

His mouth caressed my ear. "I'm getting hard just thinking about how many tears you'll cry. The pleadings for relief that will spill from your plump lips—"

My bladder let loose.

"The fuck?"

I whimpered in relief as he backed off.

"Scared the goddamn piss right out of you—"

A knock sounded, cutting Arturo off, and his touch left as I soaked the bed beneath me.

I peeked open an eye as he barked for them to enter.

His bodyguard from earlier.

"What?"

The bodyguard glanced at me and tipped his head toward the hallway.

Arturo strode away from me without a word, and the door slammed, the lock clicking in place.

My heart beat out of control, and I sat in my own piss, unmoving, zero fucks to give.

Never should have left Drew.

A sob ripped from my chest, but I willed myself to calm. I needed to focus on a plan of escape—or at least a way to keep Arturo's advances away. The Vipers didn't stand a chance against the cartel, I didn't care how bad ass or feared they might be. No one fucked with Arturo and lived.

The thought of Drew lying in a pool of blood, his body riddled with bullets tore at my mind. He might be an asshole who didn't deserve forgiveness, but the thought of being without him...

I need to get out of here.

20

DREW

We had to leave our arms at the gate—not that we'd expected anything less to gain access to Arturo's compound. The van we'd brought sat just inside the gates, our patted down and blade-stripped tense-as-fuck bodies standing alongside it waiting for an escort to the mansion. Knowing a search would take place, Vigil hadn't bothered with a two-way headpiece, including Devil in everything that went down.

He had instructions to leak the same shit Vigil held in his hands to the Feds if he didn't get a call within the hour.

It had taken the guard a quick peek in the manila envelope before he even put a call through to the main house.

Took us fifteen minutes, but Arturo himself, the fucker, strode down his driveway in the rising sun's rays, a wool coat buttoned clear up to his chin, two huge fuckers flanking him, automatic weapons in their hands.

My body itched to explode, go bat shit crazy on his ass and demand he give me back my woman, but I held myself in check, adrenaline pumping and ears buzzing as my breath puffed white clouds in front of my face.

"Chill the fuck out," Stone muttered from beside me, his stance seemingly relaxed.

He'd be in a different frame of mind if it were his woman locked up in the damn fortress before us.

Arturo stopped a good fifty feet away, his focus roaming from one of us to the next until he got an eyeful. "What can I do for you gentleman?" he asked, his voice raised.

"You have something of mine," I said.

"That a fact?" His smirk twisted his scarred mouth.

"Shaun Thode is under the Vipers protection," Vigil said, and I inhaled until it hurt.

"Who?"

"Don't bother playing, Arturo," I said, pointing to the file in Vigil's hand. "We've got the proof—along with a pile of other shit you might want to take a look at."

Arturo nodded to one of his bodyguards, and the man approached us to retrieve the evidence Devil had compiled to help persuade him to give us what we wanted.

I focused on keeping my breathing even, clenching and unclenching my fists to relieve some of the tension riding me.

Arturo accepted the envelope and slipped it open, lifting the papers out halfway before pausing. An image of Shaun in the house behind him lay on the top. That alone thinned his lips and furrowed his brow.

"How the fuck..." His voice trailed off as he flipped through the short stack of papers behind her picture, one being a listing of his contacts, another of an upcoming shipment flying into Boston that very night.

He lifted his cold gaze back toward us while shoving them back into the envelope, zoning in on Vigil. "How did you get this information?"

"Classified," I said, my voice steady and smooth as worn leather even though my insides twisted.

"And you want the girl in exchange."

I tapped the side of my nose. "Drop the vendetta

against the Thode bloodline, and we forget all about your workings in New England."

A muscle ticked in Arturo's smooth-shaven jaw, murderous intent shining in his eyes over the distance separating us. "My men could take you out at my command—and no one would be the wiser."

"I've got a phone call to make," Vigil said, glancing at his watch. "In less than thirty-five minutes. Otherwise, one click of a button lands that same information in the FBI's laps."

Arturo glared, the tension between our groups salivating my tongue to shed some blood.

"What say you, good man?" Vigil asked, a mere second before I lost my shit.

"I would say you have me by the balls at the moment," he said, his tone conversational even though his face declared him a rabid animal. He turned to the guard on his right. "Go get her."

Minutes, what seemed like hours, ticked past, my heightened breaths loud in my ears.

"What assurance do I have that this information isn't leaked regardless of our trade?" Arturo asked, pulling my focus off his front door.

"The Vicious Vipers are men of their word," Vigil said, his voice hard. "We've never had issue with your business—you've never had issue with ours. We'd like to keep it that way since we have no love for the law not in our back pocket. The last thing we want is for innocents to get caught up in a war that isn't necessary."

Arturo turned his attention on me. "Not all Vipers keep their word—their promises."

Stone grasped my arm as reflexes surged me forward.

Guns cocked, trained on us.

"I made one hell of a bad choice," I managed through grit teeth, my entire body trembling, "and it caused more pain and heartache than you'll ever know."

He snorted.

"I learned my lesson, Arturo." I yanked free of Stone's grasp and straightened. "And it cost me the lives of the two people I loved the most."

"So Ben *is* dead as his daughter claimed?"

I nodded.

"I find out otherwise, and I'll hunt every last one of you mother fucking Vipers down. Old ladies, children—I'll bury you all. *That* is my promise to you."

21

SHAUN

The door creaked open, and I sat up, swiping the drying tears from my face.

"Let's go," the bodyguard from earlier said, stepping back in the doorway.

"Why?" I asked, my heartbeat kicking back into hyper speed.

He glared at me and waited as my mind rushed over possibilities that Arturo changed his mind and told the goon to take me out back—wherever the hell we were—and put a bullet in my head. Or did he await me in a bedroom somewhere, ready with ropes to bind me and his men to fuck me until I bled?

I wasn't going anywhere without answers. "What's going on?"

"Let's go," he repeated, his voice lowering.

A battle of the wills—but the fact I'd been given an opportunity to learn my surroundings and possibly make an escape came to mind.

I scrambled off the bed, uncaring my jeans clung to my thighs, wet and smelling of piss. Head held high, I stepped into the doorway and paused, lifting an eyebrow up at him.

"Follow me." He spun, turning his back on me as though knowing I didn't pose a threat to his life.

Gray hallway. Stairs. The wooden door at the top led into a massive kitchen, even larger than the one at my dad's.

My throat tightened, but I pushed thoughts of him aside while scanning for an exit.

"This way," Goon said, striding to a revolving door.

Dining room large enough to seat close to twenty ... an entryway with a vaulted ceiling, stairs leading up to the right—but asshole went for the front door.

What the hell?

I followed him out into the cold, blinking at the morning sunlight shining in my face. Cold nipped at my nose and chilled my wet jeans to the point of discomfort before I could blink my eyes into adjustment.

"Shaun!"

Drew.

My heart lodged into my throat, and I blinked again, sure I dreamed.

Drew and a handful of his brothers stood near the far gate. Arturo and another of his scary as fuck men stood between us.

The guard in front of me descended the stairs, and I jerked forward, rushing past him, my focus on Drew. Salvation.

Safety.

Arturo didn't make an attempt to stop me as I sped past him.

Sobbing, I launched myself into Drew's outstretched arms, clinging tight as his strength wrapped around me.

"Fuck, sweetheart," he murmured into my hair. "Tell me you're okay—tell me he didn't fucking touch you."

"He didn't—but he scared the piss out of me," I said, knowing he'd smell and see the evidence soon enough if he hadn't already.

"Make your goddamn phone call, *Frankie Capone*," Arturo told Vigil as I buried my face in Drew's neck, breathing in the scent I never expected to fill my nose ever again.

"I'll do that the second we're away from here," Vigil replied, and Drew climbed into a vehicle, our chests pressed tight, our hearts thrumming against one another.

The motor started, and I finally relaxed.

"He hurt you, girl?" Vigil asked, and I pulled away from Drew, tears hazing my vision.

"No, but he's one scary SOB," I said with a shaky laugh, wiping tears from my cheeks. "Sorry I'm stinking the van up."

"Don't worry about it," Stone said from beside us, but I caught Drew's gaze and couldn't look away, couldn't thank his brothers for being so understanding—and ballsy to rescue me.

"I'm sorry," I whispered, palming the side of his face, his beard tickling my hand. "I never should have taken off like that."

"I'm taking you back home—you're mine now, Shaun." Drew rested his forehead against mine. "Nothing anyone does or says will ever change that fact."

A shuddering sigh rippled over me, and he claimed my mouth, piss stench rising from my warming jeans and all—and I fucking gave in. Gave over to the truth of his words.

I stood beneath the hot spray of Drew's shower, my head tipped back, eyes closed as he nuzzled my neck. There hadn't been a need for words when we'd arrived home, but I'd grasped his hand and led him into the bathroom. We'd stripped and stepped in, Drew's gentle touch washing me from head to toe.

No longer smelling of piss and fear, I found my body responding to his scent, his stroking my skin, his cock thickening against my belly.

"Thought I'd lost you," he murmured against my mouth, his hands cradling my face. "I was ready to go in, guns blazing to set the world on fire if that's what it took to save you."

I wound my arms around his neck and pressed forward, tasting his mouth, drinking in his groan as our tongues came together.

He lifted me without effort, his hands on my ass, my back against the cool tile as my blood heated. "I need to be inside you," he murmured, his cock trapped between us, jammed against my clit.

I had questions, but they could wait. "Then shove your cock inside me."

"Goddamn, woman." He groaned and shifted me

in his arms. One thrust seated him deep and ripped a gasp from me.

"Shaun…" Drew claimed my mouth and fucked me like the world's end lay seconds away, his arms a vise around my back, sucking my breath and all rational thought from me.

I came around him, shuddering and crying out his name—but he stopped short of releasing inside me and pulled out.

"Want you in our bed, sweetheart."

Shaking from my climax, I needed help as he set me on my feet.

Seconds later, I laid back on the bed, and he stalked forward like a feral animal, crawling over me on his hands and knees. "Your pussy belongs to me." He grasped my leg and lifted it high, rubbing the back of his hard cock over my slit. "This hole." He shoved in, bowing my back off the mattress. "This ass." He squeezed a cheek until it stung. "This mouth."

He claimed the last, and I gave it willingly, clinging to his back with every bit of strength I had, desperate to show him how much I appreciated him. Needed him.

———

Darkness coated the sky, and still we laid in bed, my cheek on his chest, my body worn the hell out. He'd claimed all three of those holes he'd said belonged to him, only having paused once to eat a late dinner since my stomach had growled.

Peanut butter and jelly sandwiches—in bed.

Our empty plates sat on the bed stand beside the bottle of lube that had been put to good use. The room around us smelled of sex, sweat, and his luscious body wash.

I nuzzled my cheek against his hard chest, my fingers trailing down through his happy trail and back up again.

"How did you find me?" I asked, finally having had my fill and wanting answers.

"We have our ways."

"That's not an answer—and if I belong to you, as you've stated, then that makes me part of the Vipers family. I should be privy to such things."

"Club business," Drew said, his voice rumbling beneath my ear.

I let out a huff. "Fine. What'd you bribe Arturo with, because I know there's no way in hell he just handed me over without some sort of persuasion."

"We gathered enough shit on him that would put him away for the rest of his goddamn life."

"And you threatened to give it to the police."

"Pretty much, yep."

"Do all the Vipers have balls as big as yours?" I asked with a smirk, fondling said balls in my hand.

He grunted and spread his thighs wider. "Wouldn't know. I don't play with my brothers' balls."

"Mmm." I squeezed and released, sliding my hand up over his semi to the ripple of his lower abs. "If you hadn't come for me when you did, Arturo would have started a war with the Vipers."

"Why do you say that?"

"Because I couldn't school my features when he asked if the Vipers had hidden me for Dad."

Drew caressed my arm absently as silence settled over us for a few minutes. "Well, no need to worry about the what-could-have-happened shit like that," he finally said. "You're here. You're safe."

I heaved a sigh. "I've got a million other things to worry about—including what to do about my dad."

"We have his body."

I jerked upright, searching Drew's face.

"The other bodies we got rid of." He glanced away, his eyes troubled. "But we weren't sure what you'd want us to do."

"I-I don't know," I whispered, the sandwich churning in my stomach. "Can I see him?"

Drew grimaced, his hand rising to stroke my hair hanging over his chest. "I'll take you to him—if that's what you really want, but it's not pretty, Shaun. I don't want the image of what Arturo's men did to him haunting you for the rest of your life."

My throat tightened. "I need to see him, Drew," I whispered. "Need that closure."

He nodded and finally lifted his focus to my face, the pain in his eyes stealing my breath. "I need to confess... There was nothing I could do for him."

"You told me that already."

Drew cupped my face in his hands, his searching gaze accelerating my breath and sending a rush of heat—not the good kind—through me.

I held perfectly still, knowing whatever he was about to say wouldn't be good. "What?" I managed.

He caressed my jawline with his thumb. "I'm the one who ended his life, Shaun."

My heart stuttered as I stared.

"I put a bullet between his eyes at his request. I ended his pain, his suffering."

Sudden coldness slammed into me, and I jerked backward, scrambling off the bed to stand on weak legs. Drew reached for me, but I backed off, holding up my hand, my ears buzzing. "You killed my father." My voice shook like hell as a slew of emotions rose to choke me.

"There was nothing I could—"

"You fucking killed my father!" I shrieked, tears hazing my vision of his face. My hands fisted, and I shied away as he sat up.

"Shaun, listen to me—"

"No." I shook my head, and turned to grab one of his t-shirts off the floor, my heart breaking all over again in the kind of grief I was too young to know so damn well. "Not right now, Drew." My voice caught on a sob, and I yanked his shirt over my head. "I-I need time to think. Need space."

He sat on the edge of the bed. "Where are you going?"

"Downstairs." I couldn't even look at his face as I rounded the foot of the bed and grabbed the pillow across from him. "Couch. I can't sleep up here with you tonight."

"Okay, Shaun." He sounded defeated. Broken, thank fuck, but he'd brought it on himself.

I stumbled down the stairs, lower lip between my teeth to keep from sobbing. I had wanted to break his heart—and he'd done worse to me in return.

Drew had promised to bring my father back to

me, but he'd taken his life instead. Dad had still breathed—there *must* have been hope. Drew should have done the right thing and called for an ambulance even if he didn't think Dad would make it.

I didn't care that Dad had asked him to end his suffering. He shouldn't have done it. Drew Tellier was not God. He had no right to take my father away from me, especially since he'd taken my mom away, too.

Not true.

I pushed against the thought, the guilt that threatened to double my grief. Yes, I'd run off that day at the park, but if Drew had been there, I never would have attempted to gain a few minutes of freedom in the pines.

His pillow soaked beneath my face as I lay curled in on myself on the couch. Thoughts and emotions kept me from sleep. I wanted a bottle of wine. I wanted darkness to take everything away. I needed a hug. Comfort and affection. A shoulder to cry on— and with the thought of Drew holding me like I needed twisting my stomach, I did the only thing I could think in that moment.

I snuck up to the office and called Krystal.

DREW

I gave her the space she'd asked for again—and it fucking killed me. The pain on her face felt like the knife in my chest, the memory of how my confession hurt her like a fist twisting the goddamn blade deeper. I didn't deserve her forgiveness for what happened ten years earlier, and I sure as hell didn't expect it for taking her father from her as well.

Shaun had been tossed into my life for a second time, a second chance to make things right—and I'd fucked it all to shit. Even knowing Ben wouldn't live another five minutes as I'd stood before him...

I'd done as he'd asked. Ended his suffering.

If Shaun had seen him, if she understood the severity of his injuries, she might think differently.

I'll tell her in the morning, I told myself as my body

tensed to climb out of bed. *I'll take her to see his body, proof of his suffering.*

She wanted space, and I would give it to her, allow her time to calm down.

My ears fucking bled as I listened to her quiet sobs and sniffles down in the living room. Jaw clenched, I stared into the darkness, needing to comfort her, beg forgiveness, and ease *her* suffering.

But I would do anything for Shaun—be who she needed, whatever she asked.

Anything, even if it fucking killed me to give her the space she'd requested.

I pulled my pillow over my head and relaxed one muscle at a time from my toes to my eyelids and back down again. Drifting off came easier than expected, and I welcomed the mindless peace.

———

I woke with the pillow still over my head.

No sound came from downstairs, but I glanced at the clock and seeing it only read six, I stayed put, allowing Shaun more time to sleep. While waiting for her to wake, I took advantage of my fresh mind, thoughts unhindered by emotion for the moment.

Figuring out a plan of attack—of explanation,

begging for a chance to make things better between us, came easy even though I hadn't guzzled my three cups of morning coffee.

By the time seven rolled around, my stomach wanted food, and I needed to take a piss.

I snuck across the hallway and took care of business, but paused at the head of the stairs.

Silence still reigned below, but I needed coffee and food.

Halfway down the stairs, the couch came into view. No Shaun.

Scowling, my heart thumping, I flew down the rest of the stairs, praying like fuck she'd gone to the kitchen.

No such fucking luck.

"Shaun!"

She didn't answer, but I hadn't expected her to.

Cursing, I sprinted up the stairs to the office. No note rested on my desk, but a quick check on my landline showed she had called Krystal a few hours earlier.

"Fuck." I scrubbed a hand down over my face, my goddamn head and heart torn in two.

She needed space, I got that, but if Arturo knew she'd taken off and was no longer directly under the

Vipers' protection, fuck knew what he'd do. I didn't trust the fucker one bit.

Jaw aching from clenching my teeth, I got dressed, grabbed my cell to try Krystal.

No answer and no surprise.

I called Stone while stomping down the stairs. "She fucking did it again."

"What?"

"Called her friend and took the fuck off in the middle of the goddamn night."

Stone cursed quietly. "What happened?"

I told him about what I'd confessed, to which he called me a dumb fuck.

"I had no choice," I growled. "She insisted on seeing Ben's body—she'd see the bullet hole. She knew he'd been alive when I found him."

"Fuck."

"No shit."

"Call Krystal?"

"No answer."

I focused on making coffee—needed a clearer head.

"We going after her?"

"Sure as fuck are," I grumbled, grabbing a travel mug from the cabinet above the coffee pot.

"And if she doesn't want anything to do with you?"

I paused, not even having considered us *not* having a future. A scowl dented my brow. "Then I'll tie her the fuck up and bring her back here."

Stone chuckled. "Can't do that, brother."

"She's mine—fucking watch me."

He chuckled some more, deepening my scowl. "See you soon, I take it?"

"Got that fucking right."

Five minutes later, I backed out of my garage, coffee in hand, anger and fear still brewing in my stomach. The sky mocked my dark, threatening mood by shining sun in my eyes as I drove down the driveway. Even warmth had returned to kiss the gentle breeze fluttering the dead leaves still clinging to their branches.

They would without doubt fall before the end of the month, but I wasn't about to allow the love I'd just found die as easily.

Love.

Lips pursed, I considered the word. Shit about not being able to protect those I'd loved in the past scraped like nails on a chalkboard in my brain, and a shiver slid over me, an ominous *fucking* feeling.

I'd failed the first woman I'd loved, cursed myself

hundreds of times, wishing I'd been the one who ate the bullet that ended her life that day. Well, I would get it right with her daughter. With the woman I found myself falling in love with.

Well, fuck that *something* in the back of my head.

I wasn't about to let a goddamn thing happen to her, and if that meant saving her from herself, then by fuck, I'd do it.

"Even if it takes ropes and a gag," I muttered, pulling into Stone's driveway.

23

SHAUN

It had been Krystal's suggestion to find someplace my head would stop swirling with bullshit—and float in who-gives-a-shit-land. Not even noon and I had a good buzz going, well on my way to forgetting the mass of muscle and tattoos I couldn't get out of my mind.

A friend of a friend of a friend, or some such bullshit, was banging a frat boy president, and they had an all-day party going on. It seemed more an all-weekend long party that dragged on into the middle of the week, the stench of spilled, stale beer and empty bottles and red plastic cups littered the entire downstairs.

Music blasted, a handful of guys played beer pong, others shooting pool at two of the tables in the huge living space of the fraternity's old mansion. A handful of people had passed out during the night, still snoring where they lay—three on a couch, two curled up almost naked in a corner, one guy in a chair beside where Krystal and I sat, his head tipped back, mouth open—and his face a black marker doodled mess.

He'd be pissed when he woke.

I giggled at the drawing of the penis along his cheek, aimed at his open mouth, and swigged my drink, thinking the guy a fool for drinking so damn much at a frat party. All sorts of rumors abounded about that particular group, full of mischievous bad boys hell-bent on ruining women and breaking every rule. They certainly knew how to party, and they didn't skimp on sharing booze, that was for damned sure.

"Krystal!" A blond guy stumbled over and leaned down, kissing her right on the lips.

"Ew! Can you just *not*, Danny?" He tried again, and she shoved him back. "Get off!"

He chuckled and grabbed his cock through his low-slung jeans. "How 'bout you do it for me, sweet thing?"

Krystal rolled her eyes—and I laughed.

"Shots lined up in the kitchen," Danny said,

swaying on his feet and scratching his chest. "Wanna join in the fun?"

"I'm in!" I hopped up—or tried to, rather, laughing as the room spun.

"Careful, there," Danny said, grasping my elbow.

I leaned into him and reached for Krystal's hand. "Shots," I said, wiggling my fingers in invitation.

She frowned, and I laughed again. "Think you might want to take a break, Shaun," she said.

"Nope. No fucking way," I held out the Y sound until I ran out of breath.

With a huff, she got up and followed along as Danny and I stumbled toward the kitchen. The booze had taken me to a lovely place of numbness, giving me that who-gives-a-fuck attitude about Dad, Drew, and the bullshit—and I wasn't about to slow down or stop.

It was forget time because I just couldn't fucking deal anymore.

A rowdy group carried on around a huge island. Chanting and shouting as though at a football game, and I whooped and hollered along with them even though I had no fucking clue what they were doing or why.

Danny pushed his way through the crowd and tugged me against his side, one arm wrapped around my waist, helping me stay steady on my feet.

A kaleidoscope of colors lit my slow-moving eyes as I attempted to look around. My ears rang. Mouth hurt from smiling. Another guy pressed in close on my other side, and I grinned at the thought of being a slice of cheese between two pieces of bread.

Every woman's fantasy ... right? Why the fuck not fulfill that now? One would never compare to Drew, but perhaps two would. Fucker killed my dad. I'm done with him and his huge cock.

I found a shot in my hand—and tipped it back when Danny did. I'd had enough I didn't even feel the burn go down my throat.

"Thata girl!" he shouted, slamming the glass onto the counter.

Another shot, another congrats from my new friend—and the one on my other side joined in.

I swayed, drunk off my ass and laughing, pressing close as Danny's hand cupped my ass. His friend crowded in even closer—intentionally or from the press of people cheering one another on, I didn't know. Didn't care.

"Come 'ere," Danny said against my ear.

Turning put my chest against his—and his mouth on mine. A brief thought of his taste being wrong, his lips too soft, fluttered through my muffled brain, but I shoved my tongue into his mouth, pushing that shit from my mind.

At least he didn't slobber all over my face.

"Wanna take this upstairs?" Danny asked against my ear, his hard cock digging into my belly.

Grinning like a fool, I nodded, so damn drunk, I sagged against him in complete surrender even though he hadn't induced a twinge of desire between my thighs.

"Mind if Jarod comes along?" Danny nipped my earlobe. "He likes to watch."

"I don't give a fuck," I slurred, turning my head to give him better access to my neck.

I blinked—or blacked out for a few seconds—and found my arms around Danny's neck, clinging to him as he carried me up a flight of stairs, following on his friend—Jarod's?—heels.

"Shaun!"

Giggling, I fluttered my fingers over Danny's shoulders at the wavering image of Krystal at the bottom of the stairs. "I'm good!" I called back, my eyes closing. "I'm good…"

I so totally was.

24

DREW

We drove around a bit, checking to see if either girl went to class like we'd done before, but they hadn't. They weren't at the apartment which Stone and I let ourselves into once more.

My phone buzzed with an incoming call, and I put down the picture from Shaun's bed stand to glance at the screen.

"Krystal?" I barked the second I swiped to answer.

"D-Drew?" She sounded broken—same fucking shit all over again—but music shrieked behind her.

"Yeah, it's me."

"Thank fuck—I need you to come over here."

Every word slurred, and a hiccup or partial sob cut her off. "Shaun."

"What about her?" I asked, hurrying out of the bedroom and into the hall, my stomach a fucking rock. Stone stood in kitchen and I caught his gaze, tipping my head toward the sliding glass door we'd jimmied open.

"She's upstairs with a couple guys. Locked in a bedroom. Sh-she's pretty drunk."

My teeth clenched together as red hazed my vision. "Where are you?" I strode out into the shining sun, Stone on my heels.

Krystal mumbled something about a frat house —a goddamn frat party—an old mansion.

I knew exactly where they'd gone, and my fucking heart pounded in my chest.

"Get your ass upstairs, find some way into that room, and stay with her until I get there," I snapped and tossed the cell to Stone.

My truck's engine roared to life, and I peeled away from the curb, my tires squealing in protest.

Tension strung me tight as fuck, and I knew I needed to get a hold of myself before showing up at a frat house where a bunch of drunk-ass college punks tried to get lucky with every woman walking through their damn door. Especially the drunk ones

—or the ones who'd gotten something extra slipped into their drink.

"Krystal said the door's locked and they won't let her in," Stone said, and I realized he still had her on the phone, but I'd been too damn focused to hear their conversation.

"Tell her to break down the goddamn door!"

"Knock harder," Stone said again, and I seethed, ready to blow a fucking gasket.

It took five goddamn minutes, and only that short a time because I ran three lights and drove on the curb and bike lane for a hundred yards to get past slow as fuck assholes.

I pulled right up to the frat house's front door, uncaring I blocked their circular drive. The truck door slammed behind me, but I was already halfway up the front stairs.

Music blasted as I let myself in, the stink of a party having gone on too damn long assaulting my nose. I ignored the voices, the drunk bodies dancing or stumbling around, my quick scan finding the stairs off the kitchen, my feet taking them two at a time.

The blonde from the BMW stood in front of a door, banging her hand on it and sobbing, a cell pressed to her ear.

"Krystal!"

She turned, mascara tracked down her cheeks and quickly stepped away from the door. "Shaun's in there."

My hand itched to pull the gun at my back, but I held onto the final thread of sanity in the back of my mind. "Back," I barked, pushing her toward Stone, who hurried toward us.

I pulled my leg up and snapped it out with a front kick, hell-bent on breaking down the fucking China Wall.

The old door splintered inward, and I followed, shoulders hunched, my eyes taking in a sight that lit a lust for blood through my veins.

Shaun lay sprawled on a bed, her shirt gone, one guy's mouth latched onto her tit. Another asshole jerked himself while watching, his aim on her face. But the third—the fucker had Shaun's panties halfway down her legs.

"The fuck?" he said, scrambling away from my woman, his upright dick sticking out of his jeans sagging quick as fuck.

Three strides forward, and my fist crunched his nose, spraying blood as he spun. He slumped to the floor, but I'd already gone for the asshole backing away from Shaun's tit.

"Dude—the fuck man—"

I slammed him in the gut with my knee, doubling him over for an uppercut that snapped his head backward. He crumpled without a sound, but like the first fucker, I knew I hadn't put his nose into his brain.

They would live, unfortunately.

The punk who'd planned to shoot his spunk all over my woman's face stood like a goddamn deer in the headlights, dick in hand, eyes wide, and mouth gaping. He blinked, and I was on him, a knee to his groin earning me a shriek—and a grin on my lips.

"You're lucky I didn't slice the fucking thing off," I said in his ear as I held him upright.

I stepped back and clocked him in the temple. He, too, went down without a sound.

"Oh God, oh God, oh God," Krystal whispered from the doorway, but I couldn't be bothered with her hysterics.

"Take care of her!" I barked at Stone while kneeling on the bed beside Shaun, the rise of her chest all I needed in that moment.

The fucker hadn't gotten her panties off, and I held onto hope none of them had gotten their dicks into her. Lips in a firm line, I yanked her panties back up and wrapped her up in the top sheet rumpled beneath her.

"Get her clothes," I told Krystal while picking Shaun up in my arms. "And get your shit. You're coming with us, too."

I stormed down the stairs, telling myself it could have been worse—I could have caught one of the fuckers buried balls deep in my woman. Arturo could have gone back on his word and got to her first.

I'd fucked up a lot of shit in my life, but I'd gotten to Shaun on time.

I wouldn't let her out of my sight again, not until she submitted to the fucking truth of where and who she belonged to.

25

SHAUN

Warmth and softness surrounded me. Although my head ached, I breathed deep, smiling as Drew's scent flooded my nose. Just as quickly, my smile dissipated. Goddamn mind playing tricks on me even after all the alcohol I'd drunk. Even after making out with Danny ... and his friends.

Fuzzy memories flitted through my head. I'd kissed Danny before he pushed me to my knees to blow him. Jarod snuck in close for a turn, but pulled out of my numb, willing mouth as another guy, one I didn't know, crowded in.

Then what?

I clenched my eyes shut as I fought to remember.

I had hoped for roughness, maybe to even be

slapped around a little, something better than what *he* had given me.

No tenderness lingered between my thighs, so either the boys had tiny dicks, didn't know how to use the damn things, or I hadn't gotten fucked like I'd wanted in that moment.

But that moment had passed, and I found myself almost glad things hadn't gone farther than they had.

Burrowing into the pillow had my mind thinking of Drew—damn him. The soft cotton really smelled like him, and I cursed myself for even considering another cock. A stupid, immature—reckless—decision all because I couldn't handle my damn emotions.

I cracked open an eyelid. Light spilled into the bedroom from the hallway.

Drew's bedroom.

"Oh, fuck." I grimaced as my head took up pounding with a vengeance, even hurting my damn ears.

How the hell had I gotten there? He'd found me —or Krystal had called him. I imagined him storming into the frat house like a truly wicked warden, a viper hell-bent on striking everything in his path to get to me.

Did he kill anyone?

I pushed up, groaning and eyes closing. *Definitely had too much,* I realized as my feet still swayed beneath me when I slid off the bed. Trying to be sneaky as fuck, I made it to the hallway and across, intent on the toilet.

I wore Drew's shirt, I realized as I bunched it up around my waist—and I didn't wear panties. Eyes closed and head tipped back, I sat, my bladder emptying as I tried to not think too hard. It hurt my damn head.

No soreness while wiping, no blood.

Definitely didn't get fucked by the three guys I remembered being in that room with me, and definitely didn't get to enjoy Drew's cock again while passed out.

Not bothering to flush—didn't want to alert Drew I'd woken, wherever he was—I peered into the mirror. The curl had been brushed from my hair, and only a trace of makeup lingered around my eyes.

I lifted his shirt and sniffed my armpit.

Drew had washed me, too.

My chest ached at the thought of his caring for me even after all the shit I'd put him through.

Two slight purple marks lay beside my right nipple—the blond guy. Lips pursed, I checked them out, remembering he'd been all over my boobs. Dropping the shirt, I eyed myself once more in the mirror.

Stupid. A goddamn mess.

What the fuck was I going to do? Drew would never leave me alone, he'd never let me go. No doubt about that fact—obviously.

A deep part of me wished for his alpha bullshit to do that very thing, but the sorrow, the sense of betrayal lingered, stirring up the war inside my pounding head again.

I'd wanted to forget him, erase the memory of his hands and body on mine with another's—and yet relief at finding myself unused beyond my mouth and boobs swelled inside me.

A shiver licked my skin.

Drew appeared in the doorway behind me, our gazes locking in the mirror. Low-slung sweats. No shirt. Hair a rumpled mess, his lips downturned as though ready to dish out punishment for what I'd done.

My pussy spasmed, wetness springing to life even while I cursed myself for being a childish fool.

I scowled, so damn annoyed by my actions, my traitorous body—and the craving for him in my heart, that I wasn't sure how to rid myself of. Did I even want to? Emotions tugged me in ten different directions, spinning my thoughts into a jumbled mess.

"What the fuck am I doing here?" I asked, the words clipped as my head throbbed, my temples feeling like they were split open.

"I found you laid out like a goddamn feast on some assholes bed—and three of them readying to take what they wanted from an unconscious woman. What the fuck were you thinking drinking like that, Shaun?"

Going with pissiness because it was the easiest to grab hold of, I tilted my chin and huffed, snatching up the toothbrush his whore friend Tina had brought for me. A squirt of paste lined it before I answered. "I was trying to forget the shit of my life the last couple of days—trying to forget you."

He grumbled about irresponsibility, putting myself in situations I might regret for the rest of my life while I scrubbed my teeth, pretending to ignore every word he spewed out of his mouth, even though he spoke absolute truth.

But beyond the wanting to forget Drew and his touch, I'd been desperate for comfort. Love. Affection in a form other than the one I craved from the man who had killed my father.

Drew killed my father.

I spit and rinsed, and swallowed down a couple of pain killers from his medicine cabinet before finally turning to face him, my arms crossed. "I don't need another babysitter, Drew. I'm not your burden for your past sins, and I'm actually not even interested in burdening you with *more* guilt, funnily enough. And I sure as fuck don't want you to be my daddy because you couldn't tell the real one no when he asked you to kill him."

A heartbeat later, I found myself against the wall, Drew's hand tangled in my hair, the other caging me in. My pussy pulsed happily, even though lingering pissiness quivered my muscles.

"You feel like a *burden*? Think I'm only in this out of guilt?" he asked, the wrath of hell in his eyes as he stared me down. "I fucking claimed you for real, Shaun. You belong to me because *I* want you, not because a man we both loved asked me to take his place in your life. You're *mine*."

Drew's tone had me grasping for a retort, but he went on before I could utter a sound.

"I didn't save Joanna. I couldn't save Ben. But I'll be damned if I sit back, leave you unprotected, and possibly miss out on the chance of having a future with you. You're my goddamn second chance at enjoying the hell out of life—and I'm never letting you go."

I tried for a haughty look even though his words struck deep in my soul, igniting those licking flames and warm fuzzies. "What if I don't want *you*?" I found myself saying, wishing to stay in bitch mode even though my anger toward him faltered.

He slipped his hand beneath the hem of his shirt and palmed my bare pussy. Of course, my thighs naturally widened, giving him free access to slide two fingers deep inside my sopping core. I couldn't deny him even if I'd tried.

A slight smirk lifted his lips, and he pulled his fingers out to shove them in his mouth. "Tastes like you do," he growled the words the second his fingers popped from between his lips.

I hauled back an arm to smack him across the face, but he grabbed my wrist and smashed his mouth to mine, stealing the curses I'd planned on spewing—and my breath.

My heart, I knew, was already gone, but that didn't mean I'd give in willingly to the bastard.

26

DREW

Shaun bit and scratched me like a goddamn coon cat, but she didn't fight to escape. The second I palmed her ass, she hopped up, wrapping those goddamn legs around me, her pussy leaving a wet streak down my lower abs as she slid to settle low on my waist.

The need to put my scent on her, my mark, covering what those three fuckers had done to her, swelled inside me like a goddamn nor'easter, and I pressed her tight against the wall, grinding my dick against her pelvis.

They hadn't stolen anything from her as far as I'd been able to tell—but I still felt the need to take back. "Any of those bastards fuck you?"

"No."

"Take out my dick, sweetheart," I said, nipping her lower lip.

She panted, all minty-fresh breath against my mouth, shoving her hand between us. "Hate you," she whispered the lie while grasping my aching dick.

I groaned, my eyes rolling back in my head. Patience gone, I held her with one arm and used the other hand to shove my sweats down.

She lined me up.

I thrust, grunting as her tight heat clasped around me.

"Drew..." she groaned, and I took her mouth again, holding nothing back, my hands bruising, my ass clenching hard with each thrust into her body.

"No fucking frat boys will ever put their dick in you. You're mine," I growled against her lips. "Say it, Shaun." I thrust deep, and she whimpered, her fingernails digging into my shoulders as her head tipped back. "Tell me you're mine."

She opened her eyes—fucking blue as the sky, pupils blown wide, and met my stare. A war of pride, hurt, and lust shone in their depths. "Damn you."

I slammed into her again, pulling a gasp from her parted lips. "Fucking say it!"

Wetness glazed her eyes, and although tension strung tight between our bodies, she gave over to my demand to speak the truth. "I'm yours." Her body bowed in my arms as she cried out, her pussy squeezing the life out of my thrusting dick.

"Fuck, yes." Wetness soaked my shaft, dripped off my balls, and still, I slammed into her, drawing out her climax. "Come all over me, sweetheart. Yeah."

Fucking flying high, I grunted once—twice—buried myself deep against her womb, and let loose, the first shot of cum through my dick rolling my eyes closed.

She cried out again, her pussy contracting around me with every spurt of my cum.

Face buried in her neck, I groaned until finished, sweaty and winded, my back stinging from where she'd broken skin with her scratching fingernails.

Fucking heaven. The best high ever.

"This," she whispered on a shuddered sigh.

"Hmm?" I nuzzled her neck.

"This is what I needed. What I wanted. I-I knew better ... I'm such a selfish bitch." Her voice broke.

My lower body holding her against the wall, I grasped her face in my hands and kissed her slow and gentle, sealing the fate of my heart to her. Giving her everything I had, everything I ever wanted to be.

"You're mine," I told her, pulling back to look in

her eyes, hating to find sadness still pulling on her brow. "But you fucking own me, Shaun. Every goddamn thought, every emotion, every beat of my heart belongs to you."

Tears hazed her eyes again.

"I won't make you stay," I said, hating the need to allow her to choose, "but I want you more than anything in this damn world."

She hesitated long enough my stomach twisted into a goddamn knot. My softened dick slid from her pussy's slick hold, but I didn't release her.

"Confession is good for the soul, right?" she whispered, tensing my entire fucking body.

"Wouldn't know about the box with a priest thing," I replied, my tone unsure. Wary. "But getting shit off your chest to those who deserve the truth definitely lightens burdens."

She bit her lip and glanced away, but I'd already caught the guilt in her eyes.

"Tell me, Shaun," I said, knowing she needed to spill something—and no way in fuck would I allow her to keep it in.

"Those three guys..." She glanced up at me and looked away again just as quick. "They didn't take advantage of me in the way you think, Drew."

I waited, nausea stirring in my gut.

"I went upstairs with them willingly," she whispered, her eyes closing. "It was an immature, selfish fucking move. There's no excuse, and I've never been so damn sorry for something I've done in my whole life."

Forcing my jaw to unclench didn't come easy. "What happened before you passed out?"

"I-I kissed one of them."

"What else?" I pushed when she didn't elaborate and the tension still rode her shoulders.

"I gave all three blow jobs," she whispered.

My heart fucking stuttered to a goddamn stop. She'd willingly gone to her knees to suck three dicks. "The fuck, Shaun?"

"I know." Her lower lip trembled as she clutched at my arms even though I hadn't attempted to release her. "No excuses. I'm so damn sorry."

My jaw ached from clenching it again as I fought the need to throttle the damn woman. "How would you feel if you walked in on me getting a blow job from Tina?"

Shaun's face crumpled. "Like you were a cheating whore who didn't deserve my love."

I let her words sink into her own damn head, but I couldn't bring my arms to release her.

"God, Drew. I'm so fucking sorry." A tear rolled

down her cheek, and she choked on a sob. "I've been an emotional wreck since Dad brought me to you, just the damn sight of you stirring up memories of better times. Love and affection. Dad was closed off to me for so damn long. I-I couldn't bring myself to trust you because of it. I made a mistake—I d-deserve to be tossed out on my ass without a backward glance."

"You do." But I couldn't let her go. "You fucking crushed my heart, Shaun," I told her, tilting her chin up to force our gazes to lock. "But it was your heart to break. Always has been. I can't change that fact. Don't fucking want to."

She blinked up at me, her eyes wide and open, allowing me in. "Y-you don't hate me?"

"I fucking hate what you did, but I'm willing to forgive you." I grimaced, knowing I would never rid my mind of the images her confession had created. "Can't promise I'll forget, though."

She let out a heavy, unsteady exhale, and I released her chin, setting her onto her feet finally.

"You're too good to me," she whispered as I pulled my shirt up and over her head. "I'm sorry for being such a bitch all the time. I-I have a lot of anger." A huff of laughter accompanied another tear as she glanced up at me once more. "Obviously. But you make me feel like ... home. Protected. Cared for. I-I haven't had that since Mom passed. And to think I almost fucked that up…"

I kicked off my sweats, turned on the shower, and picked her back up, cradling her in my arms. The second the hot spray hit my back, I turned us sideways and set her on her feet, wrapping my arms tight around her, holding her close.

A shuddered sigh rippled her body against mine.

I kissed the top of her head. "She was a sweet, sweet woman, your mom."

"The very best," Shaun mumbled against my chest.

"And while I loved her kindness, her meek spirit, I adore your fire. I even like your sassy attitude— turns me the fuck on."

Another bit of sad laughter from her had me smiling.

"Don't change one thing about yourself, Shaun. I want you just the way you are. Just no more partying with frat boys." Anger rose, but I swallowed it down rather than spew out threats and start an argument or cause more tears. I felt we'd both had enough fucking emotional bullshit to last a goddamn lifetime.

She pulled back and peered up at me. "Thank you."

"For?"

"Loving them both. Caring for them the best you could." Pain filled her eyes, and she glanced away again.

"You okay?" I asked, rubbing my hands down her back to rest at her waist, keeping her tight against me.

"I have something else to confess."

Fuck.

I couldn't speak, so I waited for her to drop the bomb that would rip us apart for good.

"It was my fault Mom was killed that day."

Took me a second to process her words weren't about the frat boys and their dicks. My brow furrowed. "Why the fuck would you think that?"

"Because I took off the second she got me out of the car. I tasted freedom on the air and couldn't be stopped."

A rush of relief over the lack of dicks slid over me, but I hated she blamed herself. "Had I been there, you never would have run like that. You never ran from me."

She finally met my gaze again, her eyes full of

remorse. Soft and broken. "Been doing a lot of running from you lately."

"And it always lands your ass in trouble." I wanted to kiss her nose but didn't. "Well, if it's forgiveness for that supposed offense you're looking for, too, then you have mine—even though I don't believe you were to blame. Not one fucking bit."

"Neither are you." She cupped my cheek, stroking my beard. "I've blamed you for so long just to keep my own guilt away. I had every intention of making you pay. Breaking your heart." She offered a sad smile. "Pretty sure I achieved that—and my actions ricocheted big time. I'm so fucking sorry. Can't say it enough. And since I'm vomiting confessions, I might as well toss out that's why I wanted to ride your cock the first time—to make you want me so I could crush your heart under my heel."

My dick twitched at the thought of her grinding her pussy all over my length even if it had been for the wrong reasons. "And now?"

"Now, I just want to start over—if you'll still have me. I want to give into my growing feelings for you, ones that started innocently when I was a little girl enamored with her big bad teddy bear."

"Not so innocent now, though," I murmured, sliding my hand down over her ass cheek.

Shaun wound her arms around my neck and leaned up, her smile—her first damn genuine smile at me in over ten years damn near stealing my breath. "Nope. Now it's downright filthy lust for your wicked ways in bed."

I laughed, feeling like a fucking load slipped off my damn shoulders. "I'm still just a play toy?"

"Nope." She popped the P. "You're a hell of a lot more than that."

I quirked an eyebrow and waited.

"You're my protector. My rock. My ... heart's desire, not just my body's."

A fucking grin planted on my face. "I've loved you from the first time I saw you the day you were born, but the second you stepped out of that damn car with these long as fuck legs..." I lifted her into my arms again, and she locked her heels against my ass, her slick slit against the back of my dick. "Yeah. I was fucking gone on Shaun the woman."

Our lips met in a heated kiss, but I pulled back before sliding my dick into her sweet pussy again. "I'd thought fate or karma fucked with me," I told her, serious as hell, "but I wouldn't change a thing that brought us to this point, Shaun. Not a goddamn thing. Bad decisions. Deaths. I'll mourn your parents for the rest of my life right beside you—but I'm not going to live with the what-ifs since it brought us back together."

"I really like hugs." She squeezed me with her legs and arms. "They help a lot when I think about them and get sad."

I chuckled again. "My arms are yours, sweetheart. Forever, if you'll have me."

Her lips twitched. "I think I will—if you can put up with me while I figure out how to act like a real adult. Let go of my anger and all that bullshit."

"No problem there. Just no more running."

"No more running," she whispered. "Promise."

Tightening my hold on her ass, I lifted her enough to notch my dick inside her body. A slow, steady thrust landed me where I belonged—inside my woman, *my* heart.

27

SHAUN

The next morning, I woke in Drew's arms—safe even from myself, the warmth of his hold even keeping pain over Dad's death at arm's length. I expected I'd be a bitch more often than not, but I trusted him to help me navigate the ways of life. Growing up emotionally. Something my dad hadn't taken time to invest in.

My throat tightened, but I decided it was time to be strong like Dad always had wanted. It was time to take a stand for what I wanted and take the steps to move on with my new life since Drew had offered forgiveness for all I'd done.

His eyelids cracked open, his slow smile melting my insides, almost making me put aside what I wanted. I needed what I needed, though. No waiting.

I cupped his cheek, his beard soft against my palm. "I need to see Dad's body, Drew. I need to see why you did what you did so I can overcome wanting to be angry with you for taking him from me."

He swallowed, his brow furrowing. "It's not something you'll ever be able to erase from your mind, sweetheart. I hate the thought of you being haunted by what Arturo's men did to him, but if it's what you need..."

"It is."

"Okay." He kissed my forehead. "Let's get some coffee and get dressed. I'll call the cleaners to let them know we're coming."

"Cleaners?"

"Club business."

"Do I need to call bullshit again?" I asked, raising an eyebrow.

Drew exhaled heavily through his nose. "Cleaners as in the crew that cleans up our messes. The bloody kind."

"Figured."

"Coffee," he muttered, and I smirked.

"Coffee. And more pain killers for my damn head." I rolled off the bed. "Never drinking like that *ever* again."

"Glad to fucking hear it—or next time I'll spank your lush ass red."

"Red enough it'll hurt to sit?"

"Red enough you won't sit for a goddamn week."

"Mmm." I tossed a saucy smirk over my shoulder before slipping his t-shirt over my head. "Tempting."

"Woman," he growled, but I hurried out of the bedroom, intent on the kitchen and black nectar of the gods.

———

Turned out, the cleaners had their own spot in the Viper's compound. Drew had needed to get his president's approval before allowing me entry—and I'd thought Ryker had been a scary mother fucker. Vigil —for vigilante, Drew had told me—was a massive brute. His cold gaze sent a shiver down over me, but he welcomed me to the club as cordially as a stuffy rich prick, proper as could be.

"It's not pretty," Vigil warned me same as Drew had done.

Remembering the sicko gaze of Arturo, nothing he ordered would surprise me. Even if he hadn't been the one to hurt Dad, he'd allowed the devastation Drew had found. Guilty, in my opinion. One-hundred percent, especially since the men who'd taken knives to him no longer breathed.

"Thank you," I said, glancing over at Ryker on the office couch. "For exacting revenge since I couldn't."

"My pleasure, little girl."

Another shiver licked at my spine—Ryker thoroughly meant every word.

I glanced up at Drew beside me. "I'm ready."

Lips pressed tight, he nodded.

My hand firmly grasped in his, we walked out the back door of Vigil's office into the sun. A warm front had finally lazed its way over New England, pushing out the rainy cold. The sun kissed my cheeks and nose, and I closed my eyes briefly, breathing in the new day, the new beginning.

One eyeful would give me what I needed to close out the mess in my head, I felt sure. Then it would be time to contact Dad's lawyer. There was nothing he didn't know. Mr. Delvecchio had been Dad's lawyer since I could remember. He'd been over to dinner enough times I'd become well acquainted with the older man—and knew he could be trusted with the truth. It would be best to talk to him rather than Krystal's dad. God knew if he'd protect my privacy and the truth of Dad's lucrative business.

Drew led me to a small building at the complex's back, nestled against the fence and woods beyond.

A young guy stood in front of a huge sink in the front room, the kind in a laundry facility, scrubbing what looked like blood off his arms.

I knew better than to ask.

"Ben's body?" Drew asked, his voice low and clipped.

"Out back. Second freezer," the kid replied, giving me a quick once over. He went back to his cleaning, probably knowing I wouldn't be there without Vigil's approval.

Drew's fingers tightened around mine as we pushed through a door which led to a small hallway. The last door on the left opened into a cool, storage-type room. Five full-sized freezers lined the walls.

No fucking way...

I swallowed the rise of bile, my mind too damn active in considering what might lay within those cold, frozen tombs.

Drew stopped in front of the second on our right, squeezed my fingers, and released his hold on my hand to pop open the lock closing the white, sterile-like freezer.

I closed my eyes.

"Give me your hand, Shaun," Drew said, his tone gruff and hurting.

My hand shook as I held it out. He grasped my fingers again, and a rush of cold air licked my skin as the lid whooshed open.

Drew pulled me close, his body strung tight as he tucked me against his side with one arm.

I let out a slow exhale and opened my eyes.

Pale skin ... blue. Mangled face, missing eye, distorted forehead with the bullet hole I'd expected...

Birthmark above his heart.

My throat burned as acid licked upward. "Oh God."

I clasped a hand over my mouth, determined to keep my coffee down—tears poured from my eyes as my gaze wandered down over the rest of his body.

Dad's stomach had been sliced open, his guts ripped apart. Missing fingers and toes—and the fuckers had even sliced his penis off.

A whining keen rose, and I turned away, coffee spewing from my mouth to splatter on the tile floor.

"Fuck." Drew slammed the lid back down and grasped my shoulders as I continued to heave onto the floor, tears and snot pouring out of me.

I coughed. Choked and coughed some more, finally straightening when I knew I had nothing left to spew.

Drew pulled me against his chest, and I sobbed, clenching at his cut, burrowing my face into his hard muscle, wishing to rid my mind of the vivid image I'd forced upon myself.

Dad was gone. Never coming back. I knew that with certainty, and the truth knifed through me until I realized it was time to get control of myself. Drew had done Dad a favor by ending what must have been terrible suffering. I couldn't even...

Be strong, Shaun, I swore I heard Dad's voice.

A few fortifying breaths and I managed to stop the tears.

"I'll need a picture," I whispered, my voice catching. "Need proof of his death—then I want you to burn the body."

"Whatever you need, sweetheart," Drew said before kissing the top of my head. "Whatever you need."

"I'm so sorry," I choked out the words that needed to be said, needed to break down the final barrier in my heart toward Drew. "You did the right thing."

Drew didn't respond, but kissed the top of my head once more, his strong arms offering me the comfort I needed.

———

Emotional exhaustion landed me in Drew's bed, but I roused myself after a few hours, needing to get the closure thing going.

I heard Drew speaking downstairs and recognized the voice of Sin, aka Dustin, who'd stayed with me when Drew had gone for Dad. Dustin had worked for Drew for a few years, but that's all I'd been able to get out of the tight-lipped man.

Rather than interrupt, I made my way into Drew's office, shutting the door quietly behind me.

Mr. Delvecchio's secretary answered. "He's in a meeting right now. Can I take a message and have him call you back?"

"This is Shaun Thode, Ben's daughter," I said, tipping my head back against Drew's chair, my eyes closing.

"Oh! Miss Thode!" the secretary's voice heightened, and papers shuffled. "Please hold on... I know Mr. Delvecchio would like to speak with you."

My brow furrowed, but I couldn't find the desire to reply.

"Mr. Delvecchio—it's Shaun Thode on the line," I heard the secretary say, her voice muffled.

Two clicks sounded on the line.

"Shaun," Mr. Delvecchio said. "Are you okay? Where are you?"

Anxiety laced his voice, and I lifted my head, straightening in the chair. "I'm safe—with my old bodyguard."

"Your father told me he left you with Drew Tellier."

I swallowed, fighting to find my voice. "Y-you spoke with dad?"

"He called after dropping you off—and he stopped by my office. I haven't heard from him—is he okay?"

"No," I managed to whisper, fighting more damn tears. "He's dead."

Silence filled the line for a few seconds, just enough time for me to steady my emotions.

"I'm so sorry, Shaun."

No words of what a good man he'd been—well respected and all the useless words people felt the need to word-vomit to grieving people. Mr. Delvecchio didn't sugarcoat or spew bullshit from what I'd remembered from his time at our dinner table. I found confidence in his character at his lack of empty lies.

"Arturo's men killed him," I said, finding my resolve once more. "I have a very vivid, graphic image of his body. It's horrible to see, but at least the fuckers didn't mess with the birthmark above his heart."

"Where is the body?"

"Gone." I clipped the word. "So what do I do next? What happens next?"

"Well." I listened to papers shuffling around. "If you'd like for me to represent you, I can file a claim to get the ball rolling."

"Yes," I answered, almost cutting him off.

"It can take up to five years to have a missing person declared legally dead, but that's not going to be an issue even without the photo, Shaun. Your father added you to everything—and I mean everything—when you turned eighteen. Bank accounts, investment accounts, every single house, and estate deed."

I blinked, noting Drew standing in his doorway, his concerned stare on my face.

He frowned, and I held up a hand as he moved forward.

"He did *what*?" I whispered.

"Everything belongs to you, Shaun. There will be no legal issues. It's just a matter of filing the claim and..."

Tears sprang from my eyes as Mr. Delvecchio's voice faded into the buzzing in my ears.

Dad.

Drew rushed into the room and knelt beside me, his gaze thunderous, but I smiled through my tears, my heart breaking and yet, happy all at the same time.

Everything is going to be okay.

I hung up a few minutes later, after setting a time to see Mr. Delvecchio in his office.

"Shaun?"

"Hold me."

Drew yanked me up from the chair into his arms and sat his ass down, cradling me to his chest. "Tell me."

I did. Everything the lawyer had said, the good, *relieving*, news he'd given me.

Drew didn't speak, and his silence tingled anxiety to life in my stomach.

I sat up, wiping at the drying tear tracks on my cheeks. "Say something."

"You're an extremely rich woman."

"So?"

He searched my face, his dark eyes shielded, almost as though he feared something. "What are you going to do now?"

Insecurity—who'd have guessed it from my wicked warden? I bit back a smirk. "Do what any woman in my situation would do."

"What's that?"

"Fuck my man senseless, then spoil him rotten."

Drew didn't crack a smile, didn't move. "You're staying?"

I huffed a sarcastic laugh and snuggled back into his chest. His arms wound around me, holding me close. My eyes closed as I soaked in his hug, his scent, his warmth—the feeling of home.

"You claimed me, so you're stuck with me, Drew Tellier."

"I'd love you even if you had nothing but the clothes on your back," he said, his breath hot against my forehead, his tone convincing as hell.

"And if I didn't even have those?"

He palmed my ass and stood, striding into the

hallway. "Then I'd lay you out on my bed and devour every goddamn inch of your body."

I clung to his neck.

"Sin!" he hollered when we reached the hallway. "Gonna be making some noise—might want to let yourself out!"

Laughter shook me in his arms.

"Right-o boss man!" Dustin hollered back up.

The front door slammed as Drew set me on my feet in the middle of his bedroom—*our* bedroom. Softness eased the lines on his face, love and lust poured from his eyes, filling up my emotionally-drained tank.

He pulled his shirt off over my head, his gaze skirting down over my naked body. "Mine," he said, brushing his knuckles down my neck, over the swell of my breast.

"Yours," I agreed, my heart finally free to trust again.

"Now get on my bed, woman. I'm going to make love to you."

I scrambled to do as told, obeying without question or argument, knowing I'd have plenty of opportunities to incite a good hate-fuck in our future—but only over petty bullshit, of course.

He stole my breath with the first touch, all thought with the second. I allowed my man to love me in the way he wanted—and I'd never been so fulfilled in my life.

THE END

———

ABOUT THE AUTHOR

Lynn Burke is a full-time mother, voracious gardener, and International Bestselling Author of hot romance books. A country bumpkin turned Bay Stater, she enjoys her chowdah and Dunkin Donuts when not trying to escape the reality of city life.

ALSO BY LYNN BURKE

Blood Born Series

Bonds of Worship Series

Darkest Desires Series

Dark Leopards MC

Devil's Outlaws MC

Elite Escort Series

Fallen Gliders MC

Found by Fate Series

Midnight Sun Series

Missing Link Series

Risso Family Series

Sandy Ridge Series

Vicious Vipers MC

Standalone Titles:

Abel's Obsession

Divulging Secrets

Healing Storms

In Between

The Playboy Bachelor